She wore baggy  of leather jack extra for becaus it to look like something a hobo has thrown away after a decade of hard use. She was lugging two suitcases.

Her face hadn't changed much since the picture had been taken.

I said: "Sarah?"

She didn't run. All she did was stand there.

"Do you know what your friends used your apartment for this morning?" I asked her.

"What are you talking about?" She looked over my shoulder and repeated her question: "What is he talking about, Henri?"

I did a fast spin-around. He was tall. He had the face to be in movies. Like Sarah, he was carrying two suitcases. Unlike her, he didn't stand there letting them weigh down his arms. He threw them at me. Something hard struck the side of my head.

When I came to, they were gone . . .

STONE ANGEL

Marvin Albert

FAWCETT GOLD MEDAL • NEW YORK

A Fawcett Gold Medal Book
Published by Ballantine Books
Copyright © 1986 by Marvin Albert

Library of Congress Catalog Card Number: 86-90881

ISBN: 0-449-12919-5

Manufactured in the United States of America

First Edition: July 1986

For two Riviera friends:

Alain Nugon,
of the Gendarmerie Nationale in Nice

&

Attorney Joel Blumenkrantz,
Deputy Mayor of Cap d'Ail
Merci Pour Tous

🔳 **1** 🔳

IT WAS THE kind of April in Paris they wrote the song about when a submachine gun began hammering at me from the other side of the Rue des Rosiers.

Paris is nothing like Chicago. Not the Chicago where I did most of my growing up, and definitely not the Chicago of the bootlegger battles that still fascinate Europe. Sometimes the same things happen in Paris, but usually for different reasons.

There'd been no response when I'd buzzed Sarah Byrne's apartment, so I'd crossed the street to have an exotic lunch before pursuing the matter further. In central Paris the sort of pastrami on rye you can get in any American delicatessen is exotic. I know only two places you can get one: Fischman's Café and Jo Goldenberg's Restaurant. Both are on the same short, narrow street in the Marais quarter, in the heart of what was a small Jewish ghetto as far back as the twelfth century.

It seemed a funny place for an American girl of Irish extraction to live. But not funny-peculiar, at that point. Like most big cities, Paris has become increasingly patchwork as space gets harder to come by. There is now Tunisian shop between Fischman's and Goldenberg's, plus a chic Scandinavian boutique at one end of the street and a trendy Russian bar at the other. The old ghetto ambience is hanging on there by its fingernails.

I settled down with my beer and sandwich at one of the

little tables between Fischman's bar and the long plate-glass window fronting the Rue des Rosiers. That gave me a narrow view of the entrance to Sarah Byrne's apartment building, if I tilted my head to peek between some of the matzo boxes stacked high against the window. The barricade of boxes had been erected to prevent people outside from getting a clear view of the interior—a precaution instituted after Goldenberg's down the block had been hit by a grenade and gun attack the year before.

I had finished half my sandwich and was swabbing mustard on the other half when Little Yuri walked in. He hadn't changed in the more than a year since I'd last seen him. Still short and plump, in a rumpled suit that did nothing to make him taller or slimmer, still wearing the troubled expression of an overage student hoping to finally pass his exams but skeptical about his chances.

He spotted me and came over with a cherubic smile. "That's a great suntan you got there, Pete." He'd spent some years in the States, and his English was on a par with his French: pretty good. "Still spending most of your time down on the Riviera?"

"About half and half."

"Lucky you. So what're you doing around here?" The question seemed as casual as his first one, but it wasn't.

"Having a pastrami on rye," I told him.

That's when the submachine gun cut loose outside.

The window exploded in at me, along with bullet-shredded boxes of matzo. I dived for the floor and tried to burrow into its black and white tiles. Shards of jagged glass rained on top of me. People began screaming, both inside and out on the street. The submachine gun kept hammering, the bullets lashing the café's interior from the front toward the dining alcoves in the rear. A series of bursts overturned tables and chairs, punched holes in the take-out counter and bar, disintegrated bottles and ripped through tin trays loaded with pastries, thudded into walls and smashed tiles.

Yuri had fallen beside me and for a second I thought he'd been hit. Then he rolled up on one hip and tugged a Beretta 92 pistol from inside his jacket. I doubted that the French government would give somebody like him a permit to carry a concealed weapon. But what French law permitted and what French cops tolerated could, like medical theory and practice, be light-years apart. The government had been letting Arab agents get away with murder for the last few years. Some cops compensated by ignoring the activities of shadowy Israelis like Yuri.

The bullets were coming in at a downward slant. With the side of my face pressed to the floor tiles I could see the snout of the weapon angling from a second-floor window across the street. The shooter was hidden in shadow behind it.

Sarah Byrne's sublet was in that building: same floor, same side.

Abruptly, the barrage stopped—for about three seconds. Then it resumed, swinging in the other direction this time, raking the inside of the café from the rear toward the front.

Yuri got his feet under him and launched himself toward the front door, leading the way with his Beretta and going fast enough to stay ahead of the submachine gun bursts. I stayed prudently where I was. First of all, I didn't have a gun. With or without one, I wasn't crazy enough to charge out into the open against a submachine gun operating from a prepared vantage point behind cover. Men like Yuri have careless survival instincts—one result of growing up surrounded by enemies who outnumber them thirty to one.

He barged out the door, snapping off two fast shots as he vanished into the street. I saw both bullets kick stone dust from the wall just below the second-floor window. The weapon up there jerked back out of sight, momentarily quiet again.

Walt Fischman popped up from behind his checkout counter with a Colt .45 held in both skinny hands. He was jumping for the door when the submachine gun let go another long burst. He kept going, out onto the sidewalk. People who survived childhoods inside Nazi death camps are another breed tending toward fatalism about mortality.

A woman lay against the base of the bar, moaning softly, her face slack with shock. One sleeve of her blouse was bullet-ripped and drenched with her blood, but she wasn't aware of it. She was staring down at the little girl she was holding. An overturned table hid most of the child from me. All I could see were two thin, sprawled legs, not moving.

I crawled to them. When I got around the overturned table, I saw there was nothing I or anyone else could do for the little girl. Not in this life. Concentrating on the mother, I ripped away her sleeve. A bullet had torn her upper arm. It was bleeding profusely. I began fastening the sleeve as a tourniquet above the wound. She didn't notice, continuing to moan as she cradled the dead child with her good arm.

A little old man crawled over and asked politely, "Are you a doctor?"

"No," I told him, "but—"

"I am," he snapped. "Get out of my way."

I let him take over, being careful as I turned away not to let my eyes drift to what had become of the child's head. I was still dizzy from the one brief glimpse.

The gunfire outside had stopped. All that was left were the sounds of shouting, crying, screaming. I got up and walked out the riddled front door. A stupid thing to do. The shooting could have broken out again right then. But I was having trouble thinking straight.

Walt Fischman sat in the near gutter, cursing as he tightened his necktie around his bleeding thigh.

"Yuri?" I growled at him.

He nodded toward the opened entrance to the building from which the attack had come. "Went in there."

Fischman's .45 lay in the gutter beside him. I scooped it up and crossed the street. I was near the entrance when five gunshots boomed inside the building. Two from one handgun, then three in rapid succession from another of different caliber. I stuck the Colt in my belt, hidden by my jacket, and began to run. Not into the building, but up the block on that side of the street.

Nobody involved in shooting up the café would be dumb enough to try escaping via the Rue des Rosiers. Too many merchants there had, like Fischman, acquired weapons since last year's strike at Goldenberg's. By now they would have them ready to use. No, the attackers would head through the interior of the block to the Rue des Francs Bourgeois on the other side. The blocks in the old sections of Paris are huge and ancient, each a miniature casbah, honeycombed by multiple courtyards, interior and exterior passages and stairways, roofs of differing heights. Mazes in which one can quickly lose pursuers.

I turned the first corner and kept running. It took over three minutes to circle the block and reach the Rue des Francs Bourgeois, panting and perspiring.

The block there was longer, with more than a dozen large attached buildings. I took up a position across the street, about halfway between the ends, turning my head to scan the many doors. People came out and others went in. More people crowded along both sidewalks, going about their own business. None seemed aware of the violence that had just occured on the Rue des Rosiers. The walls of the huge block, interior and exterior, were too thick and too numerous for the noise to have penetrated this far.

I began to feel foolish about my round-the-block sprint. There was no way to identify which of the people coming out of any of the doors might have taken part in the shooting. Nobody was likely to come out this side still carrying a weapon in plain sight.

One of the buildings I had under surveillance was the Hôtel d'Albret. Back in the seventeenth century it had been the palatial residence of the favorite mistress of King Louis XIV. Now its interior was being gutted for extensive restoration as an office building. All of its windows and doors were boarded up except for a wide opening used by workmen pushing wheelbarrows of debris out to a dump truck. The fifth or sixth time I glanced that way, a figure came out dressed differently than the demolition workers: skintight Levi's and stylish denim jacket, shiny black boots and a motorcycle helmet with a bubble visor that concealed head and face. The figure was tall but unmistakably female: narrow waist, full bust and hips.

The concealing helmet was not necessarily suspicious. Motorcycles are a popular means of transportation in Paris, used by everyone from students to attorneys who have to make swift trips between offices and law courts without getting stuck in traffic. Helmets are legally required, and that style was in vogue.

The Air France flight bag she was lugging in one hand *was* big enough to hold a submachine gun if its stock was folded. But it was also the right size for a load of books or anything else heavy you might think of.

She stopped at the curb behind the dump truck and two motorcycles roared past me, coming to a halt in front of her with their motors idling. Both drivers wore similar helmets. The tall woman swung on behind one of the drivers and leaned her helmet against that of the other driver to tell him something.

I looked at their license plates. Both were so smeared with dirt they were impossible to read. I started across toward them on the diagonal, dodging cars and shouting for the three of the motorcycles to stay put or I'd shoot. By then I was almost sure they were involved in the attack. My hand was inside my jacket, ready to draw the Colt if they put up a fight.

They didn't; they didn't even glance back in my direction. Both motorcycles screeched away from me, swinging around the dump truck and speed-weaving off between slow-moving cars.

I left the .45 in my belt and brought my hand out empty. There were too many people around who could get hit by a bullet that went on through any of my targets. Even without that hazard, *almost sure* was not sure enough for killing. So I just stood there feeling useless and watching them disappear. Motorcycles are the best getaway vehicles in a crowded city. There's no way a pursuit car can catch one through heavy traffic, or even tail it for any distance.

People who were close enough to have heard what I'd shouted were staring at me, uncertain if I was dangerous, just a nut, or some new kind of street entertainer. I grinned reassuringly and turned into the working entrance of the Hôtel D'Albret, leaving the gawkers behind. Most city people are predictable: too busy with their own intestines to take much time off for satisfying idle curiosity.

I met Yuri coming through a partially demolished interior wall, his right hand out of sight in his jacket pocket with the Beretta. "Did the other one come out here?" he asked, not at all surprised to see me there.

The other one—that probably meant he'd gotten whoever else had been part of the attack, somewhere inside the guts of the big block—the one the second motorcycle had been waiting to pick up.

"Tall girl," he added quickly. "Long black hair, long sharp nose, carrying an airline bag and a motorcycle helmet."

"She was wearing the helmet when she came out," I told him. "Took off on a motorcycle."

"You didn't move fast enough to stop her."

"Afraid not."

"Get the motorcycle's number?"

"No."

"Wonderful. I can see why the American police fired you." Yuri's eyes narrowed on me. "Okay, what *were* you doing around there?"

"Nothing of interest to you. I'm just looking for an American for her parents, and she happens to live in this neighborhood."

"Where, exactly?"

"Concentrate on your own problems, and let me take care of mine." Harry and Maureen Byrne weren't paying me to get their daughter into worse trouble than she might have already managed for herself.

Yuri's eyes narrowed a bit more. "Couldn't she by any chance be the girl I was chasing?"

I shook my head. "Mine's short, with a tendency to plumpness. Light brown hair, not long, and a snub nose."

"What's her name?"

"Not your business."

"You're one hundred percent sure of that."

I wasn't, so I changed the subject: "Think it was you they were gunning for?"

"I doubt it. People who know what I am are professionals. Mostly with Arab hit squads. The woman you let get away didn't look Arab. Her partner definitely wasn't. And any real pro would have tried for me just before I went into the café or waited until I was coming out. No, this was random carnage by some homicidal anti-Semites having a little fun. Like last year all over again."

There'd been a spate of such attacks around the time of the one at Goldenberg's by several small French neo-Nazi bands: a Jewish kid stabbed on a train by three thugs wearing swastikas, a Dutch tourist who had both of her legs blown off by a bomb near a synagogue in the Latin quarter. The worst had been a car explosion outside a synagogue near the Arc de Triomphe that had killed four people and injured thirty.

"You figure this was one of the same extreme right groups?" My question wasn't idle curiosity, and he didn't exactly answer it.

"Fanatics of the right, fanatics of the left—it's getting hard to tell the difference between the two lately."

"Let me know if you find out."

Yuri gave my request some thought. "Sure. Right now I'd better get lost."

"I'd advise it." By now police of all kinds would have converged on the Rue des Rosiers. It wouldn't take some of them much longer to work their way through the block to this side.

"I'll be in touch. Maybe about this American girl you're looking for." Yuri strolled out into the street, joining the crowds and drifting away. I gave him thirty seconds and then headed back around the block.

2

TWO AMBULANCES WERE pulling away from Fischman's, sounding their hooters to move people who were milling around in the middle of the street. There were a lot of them: indignant locals, curious passersby, police, reporters, photographers, television crews. Two cops were stationed at the entrance across from the café to keep out the news media. I was asking one of them who was in charge when the answer emerged from Fischman's Café and cut across to me.

"I thought you were down at your house in the south."

"I got back yesterday," I told him.

Commissaire Jean-Claude Gojon was with the Brigade de Récherches et d'Intervention. That's the police brigade assigned to very big crimes or ones that might prove politically delicate. He was in his late thirties, small and slim, intellectual and aristocratic, with black-rimmed glasses and soberly expensive tailoring. Very few French cops work their way up to officer rank from the bottom. Most officers start as officers, if they have the qualifications. Gojon had those: top family, law degree, technocrat brain, political agility.

"According to Monsieur Fischman and his wife, you were in their place when it happened. Why?"

"I was hungry."

Gojon's thin lips got thinner. "For information as well as food. You showed them a photograph of a girl named

11

Sarah Byrne''—he indicated the building from which the attack had come—''who has been subletting an apartment here for the past six weeks. They told you she sometimes eats in their café but hasn't been seen for the last couple days.''

''They also told me she's a nice, quiet girl. A bit shy, not much of a conversationalist. So?''

''Let me see the photograph.''

I took out the picture of Sarah Byrne. Commissaire Gojon studied it. She had a round, wide-eyed face and light brown hair cut short and spiky, semipunk. The face was pretty but not yet fully formed; some of the baby fat hadn't dissolved.

Gojon stuck the photo in his pocket. ''I understand you still keep your old apartment here in Paris.''

I nodded. I didn't wonder how he knew. When you function as a private investigator in France, you expect the authorities to keep tabs on you. Especially if you're a foreigner whose work permit is subject to official review from time to time. As an American, that applied to me.

Actually, I was also as French as Gojon, on my mother's side. But not legally. First, because I wasn't born in France. Second, because I'd never applied for French citizenship, though my mother would have made it easy to obtain. I hadn't for a number of reasons. Some were personal. Others were practical; there were certain advantages, in my line of work, to remaining a foreigner in France. My U.S. passport made some cops hesitate to hassle me too roughly out of fear of getting a black mark for causing international unpleasantness between France and America.

That didn't apply to Commissaire Gojon, however. He was one of those who knew that my past relationships with certain American authorities were not exactly cordial.

"I'll have the girl's picture returned to you," he said, "after we've made copies."

"Maybe you know something I don't, Commissaire. Because as far as I'm aware there's no connection at all between Sarah Byrne and what just happened here."

"We'll see. Tell me what you do know about her."

Gojon was nobody to play tricky games with. The Brigade d'Intervention is one of the roughest outfits in the French police system. Most people refer to it as the Anti-Gang Brigade and call its members the Cowboys. You don't get into it unless you're capable of taking on the most violent criminals, no holds barred. Gojon didn't look that tough physically. Which meant he had to be harder than most mentally and emotionally.

But I hedged where I could: "Nothing unusual. Just an American nineteen-year-old from a solid, high-income family. Over here to improve her French, absorb some culture, have a little fun before settling down to college and marriage. Her parents haven't heard from her in a couple months, so I was hired to make sure she's all right. I didn't have much trouble locating her here. She's not trying to hide her trail, just being negligent about keeping in touch with her family. That's all I know so far."

"Not quite all," Gojon said. "You know the place she rented faces this street. On the same floor the terrorists used."

"The shots didn't come from her apartment."

Gojon nodded. "They came from the landing next to it."

"She wasn't home when it happened. I rang her bell less than ten minutes before."

"That doesn't mean she wasn't there, only that she did not answer. The terrorists needed someplace where they couldn't be seen while they observed the café, planned the attack, and got their weapons ready.''

"There are other apartments up there.''

"We are checking those.''

"Have you checked Sarah Byrne's?''

"Not yet. Suppose we do so now.''

The two cops guarding the entrance parted to let us in. As we went through the long, partially enclosed passage- way, Gojon said, "You were talking to Yuri Suchar when it happened. What about?''

"The weather on the Côte d'Azur.''

"Any idea where he disappeared to?''

"No.''

"Mmmm . . .''

We emerged from the passage onto a small cobbled courtyard surrounded by ancient stone walls. There were four open doorways, three to different stairways, one to a back passageway. A dead man was sprawled on his back near the last. One cop was taking pictures while another was having trouble drawing an outline around the body: his chalk kept breaking in the cracks between the cobbles. Gojon led me over to them.

The dead man appeared to be about twenty-three. His jacket lapels and the front of his shirt were soaked with blood from three bullet holes in the middle of his chest.

"Fernand Claudel,'' Gojon informed me. "He belonged to FANE for a time.'' FANE, the Federation for National and European Action, was one of the most virulent of the French Nazi gangs. Outlawed by the government the pre- vious year, it had simply changed its name. Now it called itself the European Nationalists Group. "But according to rumor,'' Gojon went on, "he switched some months ago to one of those little organizations so far to the left that even the Communist Party can't stand them."

I was reminded of what Yuri had said.

Gojon's polished shoe made a small kicking movement in the direction of a Browning automatic lying on the cobbles near Fernand Claudel's outstretched right hand. "Two shots fired from that." He pointed a manicured fingertip at the dead man's chest: "That could be Yuri Suchar's work, I imagine."

The three bullet wounds were no more than two inches apart, dead center. Little Yuri had been a member of the Saiyeret commando that Israel had sent into Uganda to free a planeload of passengers Idi Amin was holding hostage at Entebbe airport. A basic requirement for membership in the Saiyeret is the ability to shoot very fast and straight.

We turned from the body and climbed the front stairway. There were spent cartridges all over the steps and the second-floor landing, scattered behind the open window overlooking the bullet-ridden café across the street. Police filled the corridor, taking measurements, lifting fingerprints, collecting the cartridges, interviewing tenants.

"Anybody who was home see the attackers?" I asked Gojon.

"As usual, no. People who hear shooting that close do not open their doors to look out. Sensible, even if it makes more difficulties for us." He summoned a uniformed cop and told him to open the door to the apartment Sarah Byrne had sublet.

There was a card tacked to the door with the name of the apartment's owner: Nathalie Ronet. Sarah Byrne hadn't added a card of her own. Or if she had, she'd since removed it.

The cop had the door unlocked in less than twenty seconds. I followed Gojon inside. The living room and bedroom were overcrowded with heavy furniture from another era. The windows, like the one on the landing outside, looked across at Fischman's Café. None of the rooms contained any evidence that the terrorists had used the place. We also failed to find anything that might belong to Sarah Byrne.

"She appears to have moved out," Gojon mused.

"Or she packed her things and went off on a trip for a while. Either would fit with the fact that no one has seen her around here for a couple days."

"She could have given the keys to someone."

"So could the owner."

"Madame Ronet is spending several months with a cousin in Lyon. She is eighty-two, an age when one does not normally acquire new and violent friends. But she will be questioned, naturally."

Gojon stood in the middle of the overfurnished living room, taking a last look around, a thin edge of frustration showing. "How long will you remain in Paris?"

"Until I find the girl. Or find she's gone someplace else."

"You will notify me before you go elsewhere. Or if you locate this Sarah Byrne, of course. Or discover anything further about her. Immediately."

"You're grasping at straws."

"What?"

"An American expression. It means there's absolutely nothing in this apartment to suggest the terrorists were ever in here. So there's even less reason than before to suspect her of complicity. There are a dozen other apartments the terrorists could have watched the café from. And at least six rooftops."

"I will satisfy *myself* about that, when and if the girl is found." Gojon was angry, but more at his own professional impotence than at me. The police had never managed to pin any of the series of neo-Nazi attacks on anybody. Members of extreme-right organizations had been pulled in for questioning but released for lack of evidence. Newspapers kept suggesting that the difficulty in obtaining such evidence might be due to the fact that the membership of those organizations included a number of policemen.

Gojon shrugged off his mood and managed a small smile. "Very well, you may go now. If I need anything further I will contact you."

It surprised me. He was being too polite. He must have sensed I was holding something back, even if it wasn't much. In his place I would have squeezed harder before letting go.

Then he said, "I imagine you will be seeing your mother now that you are back in Paris."

"This Sunday," I told him, and I was no longer surprised by his diplomatic manner.

"Please give her my warmest regards."

"I didn't realize you knew my mother."

"We met last week at a social affair given by the mayor. She is a fascinating woman. Her escort was General de Montfort."

Mother and her buddies.

Down in the courtyard, Fernand Claudel was being zipped into a turquoise-blue plastic bag. I went through the front passage and across the street into the café. When nobody was looking in my direction, I slipped the .45 into the open drawer under the checkout counter where it was usually kept.

The wounded mother and her dead child had been taken

away. But on the floor where they'd been, the tiles were still wet with their blood.

I went out hoping I'd been right about Sarah Byrne having no connection with the shooting. Because if she had, I was going to nail my client's daughter to the wall, and that is not a recommended method for attracting future clientele.

3

ORDINARILY IT WOULD have been Fritz Donhoff who would have been out hunting for Sarah Byrne. Though we were still partners, I had been operating more and more out of my house on the Riviera while he held down the Paris end.

But Fritz had had to go to Munich, the city of his birth, for the funeral of an old friend. At seventy-three, Fritz had many old friends who were either dying or dead. He himself continued to be vigorously healthy, and the widow of this particular departed friend was twenty years younger, pretty, and a great cook. So while he devoted some time to consoling her, the message on his answering machine advised business callers to try my number down on the French coast near Monaco.

That's where I was at noon the day before the shooting in the Rue des Rosiers. With no reason to expect I'd be in Paris so soon. With nothing on my mind but bracing myself to deal with having to bid farewell to the woman who had lit up my life for much of the previous half year.

I was inside finishing a shower when the first of the two phone calls concerning Sarah Byrne came through. My answering machine took over after the third ring and I toweled myself dry as I walked into the bedroom. The ringing phone had wakened Maidi, but she was taking her time about getting her eyes all the way open. I stood beside the bed just looking at her for a bit.

Looking at Maidi Phillips with her clothes off had become one of my greatest pleasures. Parting with that and other joys didn't come easy. We had spent most of the night consoling each other in various ways; all of which were delicious but none of which helped to make parting less difficult.

That night hadn't included much slumber. In the morning after I made us breakfast and we had it in bed she fell back to sleep. I never seem to need as much of that as most people, and that morning I was too tense to need more of it. So I'd climbed down the hill and gone for a long swim in the sea to take the edge off knowing Maidi would be on a plane flying away from me by mid-afternoon.

What made it worse was a certain sneaky tinge of relief mixed with the pain. For both of us. We were a couple of independence-cherishing critters who had suddenly found ourselves involved in that stage of a relationship where a choice becomes unavoidable. You weigh the pleasures of becoming increasingly interdependent against the unpredictable booby-traps—and hesitate. It's a stage most couples get past, with one decision or the other. In our case, the choice had abruptly been taken away from us. By an order in triplicate from the U.S. State Department.

Maidi had been a foreign service officer at the consulate in Nice for almost two years before we'd met through a mutual fascination with rally driving. It had started at the Monte Carlo Rally and had continued through companionable-type dates between lovers. By three months ago there'd been no lovers in sight but us.

Then the State Department order had hit. She was being shifted to the embassy in Bolivia. It shouldn't have been so unexpected. That's how foreign service people move up the career ladder: by being moved around the globe. And the shift from the Nice consulate to the Bolivian embassy *was* a step up for Maidi. But we hadn't let ourselves consider it until it happened.

Maidi stretched herself lazily and asked, "Where have you been?"

"I went for a swim. Thought about drowning myself when I was way out there but didn't have the guts. So I swam back."

"If you had that much energy left this morning, I must be losing my grip."

I flopped on the bed and took her in my arms. "Not to worry—your grip is still exquisitely gripping."

She curled a leg around me and whispered against my chest: "My God, I'm going to *miss* you, Pete Sawyer."

I caressed the familiar, beloved resilience of her body. "So don't go."

"You know I have to."

"No. You *could* tell the Secretary to take his department and shove it."

"Sure, and you could dump *your* profession and come along with me to Bolivia. I couldn't keep you in the style you'd like to get used to, but we'd manage."

"It's an idea."

"The hell it is. And if you don't stop doing *that* I'll miss my plane." She glanced over my shoulder at the clock and groaned. "I've got to go. . . ." She closed her eyes and kissed me, softly and briefly. "You *know* I'll try my best to get transferred back here."

"Yeah." We both knew it could be a matter of years before she managed it—or never. Under those circumstances, any vows of fidelity would have been nonsense. We were both too normally healthy for that, and too realistic to kid ourselves. Someday we might meet again. When it happened we would see if the electricity still flowed between us. Until then we would live our lives.

She kissed me again and said in a very small voice, "Make me some coffee and a sandwich?"

"Sure." I knew what she intended, but I got off the bed and went into the kitchen without any last look back at that lovely face and sweet body. It was better the way she wanted it: with no final tearful scene.

I had the coffee perking and the sandwich made when I heard her car starting in the carport out back. I poured the coffee into a mug and added milk while I listened to her driving away up the hairpin turns of the private road to the Lower Corniche.

Then the sound of the car was gone, leaving a silence broken only by the twittering of birds in the fruit trees around the house. I ate the sandwich methodically, using coffee to help get each mouthful down. After that I stood there in the kitchen for several minutes, experiencing the full weight of a sudden utter loneliness.

I knew the feeling would lose some of that weight given a little time, and most of it given more time. Man is fortunately incapable of sustaining endless grief. Or laughter, for that matter. Nature fashioned us as creatures of seesaw moods, emotional checks and balances. Without that we'd go spinning out of the gravitational pull that keeps us sane and human. That does sometimes happen to some people. But not to you and me—not as long as we manage to hang on to the two balancing essentials: a grasp on reality and a sense of humor about oneself. Neither is any good without the other.

At the moment, however, my checks and balances were not functioning too well. In my experience, doing something unrelated helps you get over that faster. I thought about the call my answering machine had taken. But I wasn't up to dealing with somebody else's problems just yet.

So I went out to the tool shed instead.

I was outside doing a repair job on the wide brick patio that overlooked a gorgeous Mediterranean Sea when the second phone call sounded. At that moment I was on my knees, carefully cementing a last brick into an area where I'd removed a number of broken ones. The pattern was herringbone, which looks great if all the bricks are positioned perfectly but sloppy as hell if they're not. So I let the machine in my study deal with that call, too.

Answering machines are one of the few genuine contributions of modern technology to a better life. They eliminate the need for office and secretary and make hasty interruptions of congenial occupations unnecessary.

I scraped away excess cement, used a level to get the last brick set in evenly with the others, and surveyed the result with satisfaction. Maintenance of the house and its terraced grounds was long overdue. I enjoy working with my hands. That was one reason I'd begun spending so much of my time down there. The fact that I'd eventually inherit the place was the added incentive.

The house was traditional Provençal: thick stone walls and sloping, orange-tiled roof. It had been over three hundred years old when my maternal grandfather bought it. The walls had been the only part that hadn't needed rebuilding. In the municipal records of the village above, Cap D'Ail, it was still listed as La Ruyne, the ancient French way of spelling "ruin." But restoration crews had spent two years turning it into a comfortable and attractive place to live.

My grandfather had had that kind of money to spend in those days. Then his wife had died and he'd gotten the gambling fever. The Monte Carlo casino was only five minutes away. By the time he'd died there wasn't much left for his daughter, Babette, except the house.

She hadn't spent much time there after she'd turned seventeen. That was her age when she'd met my father, in the last year of World War II. She was up in the mountains by then, part of the Resistance band that had picked him up after he had bailed out of a burning American bomber. Babette was still seventeen and he'd just turned twenty when they got married. He didn't make it to twenty-one.

He was killed in the last weeks of the war, a few days after his pregnant bride was smuggled out of France, narrowly escaping the Gestapo agents who'd destroyed her band. She ended up giving birth to me four months later, in Spain.

So all I knew of my father were some old photographs and a name chiseled on a memorial column in the Maritime Alps some miles north of the house: "James Sawyer—*Sergeant Américain, 20 ans, tué par les Nazis.*" For me he would always be twenty, and I was now old enough to be his father.

I got up off my knees and went to the patio table to pour myself a glass of *rosé des sables*. The table's wicker top was beginning to shred and unravel. I would soon have to repair or replace it. The wine, on the other hand, had absolutely nothing wrong with it.

Rosé des sables means rosé of the sands—the grapes from which it comes having been grown in the sandy soil close to the Mediterranean. It's not famous elsewhere in the world, because it doesn't travel well unless you add so much chemical preservative that the original flavor is ruined. But it is the most refreshing light wine produced anywhere along the south coast. It was one of the types I considered experimenting with whenever I got into my daydream of gathering enough money together to chuck my present occupation, buy up some unused land, and get into the professional cultivation of wine myself.

That was a dream I'd had for a long time. It took on increased seriousness every time my work got me mired in some of the messier aspects of people's lives. Working the earth to cultivate any type of farm produce has its own problems and failures, God knows. But they're not the kind that make you ashamed of being a human being.

I stood there and sipped the rosé while I enjoyed the scenery below. I never got tired of it. The lush green of the densely wooded slopes tumbled down past the house to a cove protected by sheer stone cliffs. The multi-shaded blue of the sea sparkled under a hot golden sun. The view always brought nostalgia for summers spent there with my mother when I was a kid.

She had never had more than the summers to spare for it. The rest of the time she was too busy in Paris. First as a student at the Sorbonne, and finally as a professor with a growing reputation for her studies in the history and psychology of art. Accomplishing all that, on her own, made it hard to raise a kid at the same time. So after I turned five I was shipped off to my father's parents in Chicago. And during each summer's school vacation they shipped me back to spend six weeks here with Babette.

For my grandparents in Chicago I was a living extension of their dead son, my father—and they made sure I was properly registered as having been born an American citizen by virtue of being the son of an American. Babette had made that easy for them by doing the same, at the U.S.

embassy in Spain, shortly after I was born. For her, too, back in that time, I was all that was left of the young American she'd loved, married, and lost.

My own feelings about it were influenced by the fact that my room in my grandparents' house was the one my father had grown up in. In some ways I became more attached to his memory, when I was a kid, than to my mother. I grew up thinking of myself as an American, getting my education in the States, doing my military service in the U.S. Army. But I also grew up spending part of each year in France, and I wound up speaking, thinking, and even dreaming in both French and English.

I've had Americans ask if I didn't sometimes find that confusing. I didn't. France is full of exiles and expatriates who do the same and find it perfectly normal. Nor would any of them find it odd that I still thought of myself as American but felt at home in France.

Especially and increasingly, I felt most at home in the house overlooking the Mediterranean. Nowadays Babette didn't come down there for more than a few days at a time, even in the summer. Usually she was too busy elsewhere, doing research in museums or going on business trips with Serge, a shipping company executive she'd married when they were fellow students at the Sorbonne.

But the place meant more to me than it did to Babette. The cove below was where she'd taught me to swim—and where I'd finally gotten better at it than she was. I had never been able to match her diving expertise, however. Old people in Cap d'Ail still remembered watching young Babette dive off the cliffs that flanked the cove. I remembered watching her do it, too—and being scared to death each time. It was a long way down from the top of each cliff, with jagged rocks poking out of the sea waiting to crush her skull to jelly if she didn't cut the water just so. She never got it wrong. I never tried it.

Her diving skill was famous up in Paris, too. She'd celebrated the receipt of her Ph.D. by taking a dare: diving off the Pont Neuf into the river. A police launch had dragged her out before she could swim back to the Left Bank. They held her under arrest for an hour before releasing her with embarrassed apologies. When you've been awarded both the Croix de Guerre and the Légion d'Honneur you have to do something a lot worse than diving into the Seine to get into trouble you can't get out of.

I was smiling at the memories and gathering up my tools when a couple of women appeared among the palm trees and umbrella pines below, making their way down the last of the dirt path into the cove. I stood and watched them. They kicked off sandals, got rid of jeans and shirts, and stretched their sleek, nude figures out on a long, flat rock to improve their overall tans.

If we ever sold the house, the view from the patio alone would add substantially to the price. The sunbathers who used the secluded cove—whether they preferred it nude, just topless, or prudishly wearing both sections of their bikinis—were usually worth looking at. For the few houses on the slope there was a narrow private drive that hairpinned two-thirds of the way down from the road. But for people without a key to the gate up top, it was a long, steep climb down, and a much stiffer climb back up. That tended to discourage anybody who was not in the very best shape.

I'm not crazy about sunbathing myself. Solo, it's a bore. But the pair sprawled out on that rock with the surf foaming sensuously around them did have a certain magnetism.

Not enough, however. I was having too much trouble

coping with the loss of Maidi that day. You have to sort yourself out before you proceed to the next stage of trying to compensate with the distractions of other women.

Work was still the best immediate remedy. I went inside the house to check on those two phone calls.

And I got handed what turned out to be the unexpectedly hazardous assignment of hunting for young Sarah Byrne.

4

THE FIRST MESSAGE on the machine was from Paul Rochefort and the second was from his secretary, asking me to *please* call back as soon as possible. Rochefort was a business attorney who represented legal interests in Paris for international firms. One of his clients was Meacham Services Ltd., which sometimes threw work my way when its staff investigators were overloaded.

Jasper Meacham, a former Scotland Yard fraud squad detective, now ran his own company with branch offices around the world. He specialized in what had become the most lucrative line in private investigation work: trapping industrial counterfeiters who made bogus copies of everything from Chanel perfumes to Apple computers.

Fritz Donhoff considered gathering evidence against these name-brand fakers to be boring work. It could be. But it paid a good deal more than tracing missing persons, which was Fritz's speciality. And the expense account living, when you were off in places like Madrid or Manila posing as a buyer for an American department store chain, could be positively opulent.

So I returned Rochefort's call. But he hadn't phoned me for Jasper Meacham this time.

One of the other companies Rochefort represented was a booming California sporting goods firm. It was run by a husband and wife team, Harry and Maureen Byrne. According to Rochefort, the wife was the real business brain.

Her husband, who had inherited the firm from his father, functioned mostly as a good-natured front man, charming the wholesale buyers and inspiring the international sales force.

Their problem was a personal one, the kind my old-fashioned partner found most satisfying: missing kid, worried parents. But Fritz was occupied with the Munich widow, and I had finished my job of repairing the patio and required something else to pry my mind out of its Maidi Phillips depression.

What I withheld from Commissaire Gojon the next day was the real reason Sarah Byrne was in Europe. She had gotten into trouble in California and her parents had shipped her to France to get her away from unsavory friends. Two of those friends had wound up in prison for some act of criminal violence. Sarah had narrowly escaped being charged with complicity. It was all pretty vague, but that was all Rochefort knew. Harry and Maureen Byrne had been reluctant to give him details.

Their original idea had been for their daughter to move in with a Parisian family whose sporting goods chain did business with the Byrnes's firm. Included in the idea was the possibility of Sarah's learning the European end of the business. But she had eluded members of that family waiting for her at the airport and checked into a residential hotel instead. Then Sarah had informed her parents she preferred to discover Paris on her own and to make her own career decisions.

Hoping for the best, they had continued to send her a generous allowance each month through the American Express office in Paris. Her only communication with them had become a monthly postcard acknowledging receipt. But she had failed to send one after the last payment.

Her parents were now on their annual business trip to Europe, which began with a week of sales meetings in England and would finish at a convention of sporting goods dealers in Cannes. One of the places on their schedule between those two was Paris. They had planned to see their daughter there. But a phone call from London that morning to her last known residence, the Hotel Paradis in Montmartre, gave them something new to worry about.

Sarah had moved out of the Paradis six weeks ago. No forwarding address. The Byrnes had immediately phoned their Paris attorney and asked him to get them some professional help in finding her.

The job sounded fairly straightforward, and it would get me away for a while from surroundings that reminded me of Maidi. Sarah's parents were prepared to pay a healthier per diem than usual. And I owed Paul Rochefort for past favors—and, I hoped, for future ones.

I told him okay, broke the connection, and called the Côte d'Azur airport for a seat on the next jet to Paris. I phoned the Monaco helicopter service and booked one of their five-minute hops to the airport. Then I walked up the private drive to see my nearest neighbors, the Ruyters. Bill Ruyter was an oil engineer who worked for Dutch Shell's Monaco headquarters. He was in Singapore that week dealing with a shaky offshore rig, but his wife, Judith, promised to keep a check on my house and make sure the garden and fruit trees got enough water while I was away.

I was back in the house packing my bag when the phone rang again. This time I picked it up.

It was my mother, calling from Paris.

I said, "Welcome back, Babette. How was Philadelphia?"

"More stimulating than its reputation," she told me. She'd been spending a semester there as a guest professor at the University of Pennsylvania. "I've been back almost two weeks and haven't been able to get you on the phone."

"I guess you're the one who keeps hanging up every time my answering machine cuts in. Why didn't you leave a message?"

"You know how I hate to talk to those machines."

I let her hear my sigh. "Okay. How is Serge?"

"Serge is fine except that he had to fly off to Brazil this morning to take care of a company emergency. That leaves me without an escort and I'm invited to a luncheon reception at the Elysée on Sunday for some of the old Resistance people. In addition to which I haven't seen you in months and I've missed you. If you *could* come up to Paris I'd appreciate it."

"If you want me I'll be there," I told her gallantly. I didn't mention that I'd be in Paris anyway. "I never refuse an invitation from a beautiful girl."

Babette chuckled. "You are a nice boy."

It was a long time since I'd been a boy, but I enjoy flattery as much as she does.

One of the handy aspects of the Riviera is having an international airport that can get you to any part of the world without too many changes of plane en route.

The flight up to Paris takes only an hour and fifteen minutes. Less time than most people spend commuting into any big city from their homes in the suburbs.

The apartment I kept in Paris was next to Fritz Donhoff's in one of the solid old houses inside a cobbled courtyard half a block from Place Contrescarpe. I left my bag there and walked two blocks to the garage where I kept my Paris car, a three-year-old Renault 5. Then I spent what was left of that first afternoon in Paris making the basic inquiries.

At American Express I found out that Sarah Byrne had picked up her last monthly allowance and hadn't left instructions for the next one to be sent anywhere else. At the Hotel Paradis, nobody had any idea where she'd moved to nor anything else of use about her. A check of Montmartre bistros nearby didn't turn up a single person who knew her by name.

I finished off that workday with a friend in the documentation center of the Paris Prefecture on the quai des Orfèvres. It took a while for him to make sure of the bad news; if Sarah Byrne was still around Paris, her presence wasn't registered anywhere as a resident alien—not since she had left the Hotel Paradis.

It was getting toward dusk when I returned to my apartment to phone the London hotel where the Byrnes were staying. It was Harry Byrnes who answered. He sounded like a nice guy, and he also sounded extremely troubled about my not having located his daughter yet. I told him I couldn't go much further without a picture of her, plus some information about how she liked to spend her time.

Her father said she'd often attended dance-exercise classes in California, liked to read, went to the movies a lot, was interested in astrology and tarot, and sometimes expressed vague ambitions about becoming an actress. He promised to send me a picture of Sarah via one of the private courier services that fly between London and Paris every day.

When I asked what kind of trouble she'd gotten into back

in California he was silent for a couple of seconds, and I could hear a woman's voice in the background. I couldn't make out what she was saying, and I figured it had to be his wife, listening on an extension.

"Just the usual kid's nonsense," Harry Byrne finally told me. "You know how crazy young people are these days."

His evasive tone didn't fit what he was saying. That worried me, but not as much as it should have.

I showered and put on fresh clothes and went out to dinner. Eating in when I'm alone depresses me, and that evening I had a special need for company making cheerful noises around me. So I went to Balzar, over near the junction of boul' Mich' and St. Germain. It's the most congenial brasserie in Paris, the cassoulet is excellent, and it held no memories of Maidi Phillips.

The photo of Sarah Byrne arrived early in the morning. With the picture was a note from her mother. Maureen Byrne would be arriving at Charles de Gaulle Airport that afternoon at three P.M. to talk to me. She wanted me to meet her in the airport dining room, because she had to catch a flight back to London for a meeting the same evening.

Armed with the photo, plus the tidbits Sarah's father had given me about her habits, I began hitting the places where young Americans gather in Paris. At the fourth one I found her trail.

The American Church, on the quai d'Orsay facing the Seine, has a five-floor brick annex that contains almost everything the expatriate community might need: a theater and a basketball court; classrooms for polishing one's French, picking up college credits, or learning sundry martial arts; an English-language library; and an office of Alcoholics Anonymous.

Sarah Byrne had until recently been a regular at sessions in modern dance and rhythmic exercise conducted in the annex theater.

"She was trying to slim down," the woman who had been Sarah's teacher explained. "Not that she's fat, just a tinge plump. Everybody wants to be skinny nowadays."

Sarah Byrne had also been a regular at the bulletin board in the annex lobby, where Parisians occasionally advertised sublets. She'd been tired of living in her hotel, and she had finally hit lucky: the apartment on the Rue des Rosiers. The dance teacher knew the exact address because Sarah had invited her to dinner there about a month before.

"I haven't seen her since. She told me she'd just met some 'super' boy. I guess it got serious."

She couldn't give me the boy's name or where he lived. All she knew was that Sarah had met him at a bookshop called Shakespeare & Company. There was nothing further that she or anyone else around the American Church could tell me, so I headed for the Rue des Rosiers—and wound up inside the target of a terrorist machine-gunning.

It was two P.M. when I left the street where the windows of the apartment sublet by Mrs. Byrne's daughter looked into the place where another woman's daughter had just died. I began perspiring again as I walked two blocks to my parked car. April mornings in Paris are colder than on the Riviera, and I'd put on a sweater under my jacket. But under the afternoon sun the city air was turning hot. When I reached my car I took off the sweater and tossed it in the back seat. Then I drove out to de Gaulle International.

There was just enough time left to keep my appointment there with Maureen Byrne—and find out what she really knew about her kid.

⊠ 5 ⊠

DE GAULLE IS as French as O'Hare or Kennedy. International airports are pretty much alike, and so are their restaurants. My ham omelette was unaware of the country's culinary reputation. But it filled the spot left by the sandwich I hadn't gotten to finish in Fischman's Café.

All that Maureen Byrne was having was a tall glass of Perrier. She wasn't the hard-eyed businesswoman Paul Rochefort had led me to imagine. Her eyes were soft, and so was her voice. She was a slimmer, older version of her daughter. Her suit was elegantly tailored but not trendy, her hair was cut longer than that of most French women executives, and she didn't use makeup to hide the work and anxiety lines around her mouth and eyes.

I found myself liking her. But ever since I'd made the mistake of telling her what had happened at the Rue des Rosiers, she'd been avoiding what she had made the fast flight over to talk about.

"Your name makes me curious," she said. "Rochefort told us you're American, and Sawyer fits that. But your first name—that can't be anything but French."

I got rid of the omelette's taste with a long sip of a silky Beaujolais that was distinctive enough to remind me what country I was in. It's hard to do anything very wrong with a good year's Beaujolais. "I'm half and half," I told her. "The family name is my father's. My mother is responsible for the first name."

"Pierre-Ange . . . Do I pronounce it right?"

"With Americans it's Peter or Pete. Much simpler." I am not overly fond of my French first name. It sounds fine in France, but if you're a kid in the States you try to make everybody forget it. I had grown even less fond of it later, during an affair with a girl named Moira, a fellow student at the University of Chicago. Moira had worked out the literal translation of Pierre-Ange: "Stone Angel."

She claimed it fit. According to her I was a cold bastard with a contradictory streak of human warmth—or was it vice versa? It had started as a joke, but the affair had ended with her saying she meant it.

Stone Angel—the description still bothered me as much as the name she'd translated it from.

"Then I'll call you Peter," Mrs. Byrne was saying. "And please call me Maureen. I prefer first names, in business as well as—"

"Does that mean," I interrupted, "that we've gotten friendly enough for you to tell me whatever it was you didn't want your husband to say over a phone line? Or are you going to fly back to London without giving me every detail that can help me find your daughter before the police do?"

"I am *sure* that Sarah had nothing at all to do with the terrorist attack you described." Her voice was quite steady, but the fear had peeked out of her eyes again.

I wanted her more scared than that. "If the cops get her first, they won't be gentle about finding out if she did or not. You're paying me to try to help with your daughter. The cops have other fish to fry—and I do mean fry. They're after some political murderers who'll murder again if they're not caught. I know the man in charge of the investigation. He once half killed a man he was interrogating.

With his bare hands. It was covered up, of course . . . because it turned out the man was guilty. But—''

Maureen Byrne's determined composure broke. ''My God, what are you trying to do to me?''

''What kind of trouble did Sarah get into in California? Tell me or find somebody else to look for her.''

''She just got mixed up with some stupid young people. From well-off families, but bored and looking for something exciting to do. A couple of them were arrested for vandalism.''

''They were sent to prison,'' I reminded her. ''That doesn't sound like simple vandalism. What were these friends of your daughter, some imitation of the Manson gang?''

''No, no . . . nothing that horrible. They had . . . they *thought* they had political motives.''

The omelette wasn't sitting right in my stomach. ''*Tell* me.''

I must have sounded desperate, because it seemed to scare Maureen Byrne more than anything else I'd said. She wet her lips with two flicks of her tongue and glanced around quickly to make sure no one was close enough to hear. She picked up her half-finished Perrier. Then she set the glass back down without tasting it and lowered her voice a little more.

''They considered themselves a newer version of the Weathermen. Called their own group the Second Coming.'' She grimaced with distaste. ''Crackpot would-be revolutionaries. Just dumb kids who didn't really have any idea what they were doing. They exploded some dynamite near a police station. At night. When no one was around. Nobody was hurt. And Sarah had nothing to do with that. The police would never have let her go if she had.''

"You mean they did arrest her—for questioning?"

"Yes . . . but they let her go two days later."

I studied Maureen Byrne's agonized expression. "I imagine you and your husband have some political pull in that state. How much did you have to pay under the table to get her out of it?"

"More than we could afford . . ." Her hands clenched into fists on the table between us. The knuckles were white. "Oh, God . . . what did we do wrong in raising her? We did our best. Even when we had business problems, we tried never to let them prevent us from giving her attention. We've had such hopes for Sarah. There were times when she was very young that we almost lost the company. But now it's very solid. And I thought, since we don't have a son, that Sarah might one day take over as head of it. I suppose that sounds odd to you. People usually think of rearing a *boy* to run the family firm, not a girl."

"Not so odd," I said. "According to Paul Rochefort, *you*'re the one who runs it now."

"That's not fair to Harry. And not true. What he does is essential to the company."

"But you run the business end."

"There wouldn't be much point in running any company unless the buyers and the salesmen in the field were injected with enthusiasm for the product."

"Your husband gives them the injections."

"Better than anyone I know."

I pushed her back to the subject: "But your daughter isn't interested."

"Sarah has always been rebellious. I don't know why. Against anything we believe in, against the business. She said she grew up seeing us worry about it all the time, and that's not the kind of life she wants. I thought she'd outgrow that feeling. Even when she dropped out of high school a year before graduation, I wouldn't have minded so much if there had been something positive she preferred to devote herself to. But instead . . . she began hanging around with those spoiled political crazies.''

"Crazies of the left or right?"

Maureen Byrne tried to shrug, though she didn't look as though she felt like shrugging. "They claimed they were on the left, but I don't know what they meant by that. I don't think they did, either. They said they weren't communists, because they felt the Soviet government had gone as sour as ours. They just wanted to show opposition, in some way, to what they considered the corruption of our government."

"A bombing is an easy way of showing it without having to think up a cure."

"The others in that gang were older than Sarah," she said angrily. "And none of them had ever had any *real* problems to screw them up. None of the usual excuses criminals give. They never had to fight their way out of an ignorant, bone-poor background like I did. They never had to work eighteen hours a day, like Harry and I did, to pull a business back from the edge of bankruptcy."

I had more of my Beaujolais and let her talk it out. It was obvious she needed to.

"I do realize," she went on slowly, thinking over what she was saying, "that *that* could be their problem. People who have to struggle to survive don't have to look someplace else for a purpose in life. But you don't need violence and danger to feel a sense of purpose."

"Some people do," I put in mildly. "Makes for good combat troops, as well as terrorists."

Maureen Byrne considered it. "I think it was more than

that for some of them in that crackpot gang. One of the boys who went to prison—he said something at his trial about wanting his having been in this world to make a difference. He said the thought that it didn't matter if he'd lived or not made him feel too empty. I suppose that's another motivation with terrorists.''

I didn't point out that the same could apply to politicians, artists, and high-pressure business types. Along with cops and saints. There's no single, simple answer to why people do things. No one key some psychiatrist can help you find that will unlock everything that's wrong in you. We're more complicated than that.

''Mrs. Byrne,'' I asked her, ''did Sarah have any contacts in France when she came over other than the family she was supposed to move in with?''

''No. That was one reason why we sent her here. To make a fresh start, meet new people, perhaps get interested in something constructive. I can swear to one thing: Sarah *never* had any anti-Semitic feelings. She hates intolerance of any kind. . . . You *don't* think she had anything to do with this atrocity, do you?''

''I'm going to try to find out.''

''Before the police? And you'll protect her?''

''I'll do everything I can for her,'' I promised. It was not a straight answer to her question, but it was the best I could manage.

The P.A. system began announcing Maureen Byrne's British Airways flight back in London. She gave me the schedule she and her husband would be following between London and Paris, with the names of their hotels in Brussels, Amsterdam, Frankfurt, and Copenhagen. I gave her my assurance that I'd phone as soon as I tracked down her daughter.

She wasn't crying when I walked her to the departure gate. But she looked as if it might have been better for her if she had.

6

ENID JAEL SAT yoga-fashion on the studio couch sneezing violently into a couple of hastily snatched Kleenex tissues. She was a stunning black girl of about nineteen, with huge eyes and crisp hair trimmed very short to show off the elegant shape of her skull. "Excuse me," she apologized. "It's all this book dust. I can go days without it bothering me, then suddenly it sneaks up and starts tickling again."

Dust is one thing Shakespeare & Company has plenty of, along with thousands of old books and a cozy commune atmosphere. It occupies several floors of a tall, narrow house on the Quai de Montebello, just across the narrowest arm of the Seine from the majestic bulk of the cathedral of Notre Dame. The bookshop has catered to generations of English-language readers, providing a meeting place for literary figures and a haven for traveling students low on cash.

Enid Jael sneezed again, dabbed at her cute nose, and grinned at me. "I console myself with the thought that I'm probably sneezing the very same dust breathed by Hemingway and Gertrude Stein."

Every floor of the shop has several rooms, most with a narrow bed half-hidden among banks of overflowing bookcases. Arrangements for free sleeping privileges in exchange for help around the shop run from overnight to a year, depending on how much the owner, George Whitman, likes any particular needy houseguest. Enid Jael's squatter's rights on her couch had so far lasted almost six months.

The couch was tucked in between display cases of illustrated books of the 1920s and backed by an old framed mirror that reflected the view outside the window. The last of the day's light was fading there. Hordes of Germans, Japanese, and Americans were trudging out of the cathedral and climbing back into their tour buses.

There were flaws in the mirror that made the scene appear to be happening in another world. The same flaws made funhouse alterations on my face and the back of the girl's head whenever we moved. She lowered her Kleenex, waited cautiously, then finally relaxed. "Okay, that emergency's over. Sorry."

Her accent might have been New York or New Jersey.

I flicked a finger against the photo of Sarah Byrne. Commissaire Gojon had been prompt about keeping his word. I'd found it waiting in my apartment mailbox when I'd returned from the airport. "According to George, you know more about her new boyfriend than anybody else in the shop. Henri Lammar, is that right? George wasn't sure."

"It's *Lemaire*. And what George means is that *I* went with Henri for a while. Back when I was new in Paris. That's what he comes around here for: to pick up foreign girls. He figures we're easier to manipulate than French girls. I guess that's true, in the beginning. You're in a strange country, still unsure of yourself. Henri likes to play guru."

George had said that Sarah Byrne used to come in occasionally to buy books and hang around the fringes of the young groups that gathered there. Obviously looking to make friends, but not finding anyone she was entirely at ease with—until Henri Lemaire. "George says you're the one who introduced them to each other."

"In a way. She saw him and asked me to. I never saw Sarah really open up with anybody before. But inside an hour she was inviting Henri to her place for dinner. He *is* gorgeous."

"I understand he's about twenty-three and not a student. What does he do for a living?"

"Not a thing. Doesn't have to. Rich family. Big in the wine business, he told me. With a lot of land somewhere out around Reims."

"Nobody here has seen either of them since you introduced them. Have you?"

She nodded, her head changing shape in the mirror behind her. "Once, about a week ago, near St.-Germain-des-Prés. They were waiting in line for a movie. I was late for a date so I didn't stop to talk to them."

"Where does he live in Paris?"

Enid Jael gave me the address.

"Think she might have moved in with him?" I asked her.

"If you mean on a long-term basis, I doubt it. Henri's out for kicks, not steady relationships. But you should have seen the way she was hanging on to him outside that movie house. Like she thinks he's God. Well, she can have him. He looks great and he's got a nice apartment, and he's not a bad lover. But his head's too creepy for me."

"What way?"

"The reason I stopped going with him. I bought him a Che Guevara poster. He put it up on his wall, and then he said maybe he should get a picture of Hitler to put up beside it. Can you *believe* that? I asked him if he was crazy. But Henri claimed they weren't that far apart in their thinking. That they were both revolutionaries who wanted to destroy corrupt governments and got martyred for it. Che Guevara and Adolf Hitler! What d'you think of that mental juggling act?"

"I don't think Hitler would have approved of his selecting you as a girlfriend."

"That's what *I* said to Henri. But he thinks the history books are a pack of lies. Henri told me that outside of hating Jews and Gypsies, Hitler didn't have anything against other races—in their place. Got that? In their place. I told him I didn't think my place was staying with a guy who thinks I should stay in my place. Abrupt end to a short affair."

"What are Sarah's political beliefs—more akin to Hitler's or Guevara's?"

"Search me. Sarah never discussed anything like that with anybody around here, as far as I know."

She rambled on about Sarah Byrne for a while, and I kept her at it with questions that probed for some useful handle on the missing girl. But Enid Jael wasn't able to come up with much more than George and a couple of the shop's other houseguests had already given me. People who get to know one another around a bookstore are like people who belong to the same chess club. Members of a club can play one another for years, greeting one another like bosom pals and arguing fiercely about techniques of play, without ever getting around to intimate information like where they live, whether they're married, what they do for a living.

At Shakespeare & Company, Sarah had talked about books and very little else. She had a new interest in science fiction and more than a passing curiosity about anything to do with the occult.

"A bunch of us once got into an argument about astrology,'' Enid Jael told me. "A lot of kooks think the stars are up there just to give you advice about your future. Sarah figured astrology should be used more as a guide to our psychological makeup than for fortune telling. Personally, I think the whole subject's nonsense. But Sarah struck me as somebody looking for something to believe in. There're a lot like that: they've chucked religion and gotten disillusioned with politics, and they feel a big need for something to take their place."

She didn't have anything more to say about Sarah, so I switched back to Henri Lemaire. But she didn't know of any militant group he might have contact with.

"Did you ever meet any of his friends who struck you as politically inclined?"

"I never met *any* of his friends." Enid Jael laughed, then scowled. "There are people like that, you know. Turned on by the difference in skin, but embarrassed to let their close friends know it."

"Does he by any chance drive a motorcycle?"

"Yeah, how'd you know?" Suddenly she sneezed again, barely getting the Kleenex to her nose in time. "Damn! It's starting again."

I gave her my business card and asked her to call me if she saw Sarah or Henri Lemaire or heard anything more about either. Then I went back upstairs to George's apartment and told him the same.

He had just brewed a pot of tea and was looking for cups, not remembering where his wife kept them. His mind was on loftier matters, like nurturing young talent and digging up enough dough for the huge taxes the government dumps on small businessmen. He finally picked up a tin cup somebody had used as an ashtray, dumped the butts in a wastebasket, gave it a fast swish under the faucet, and filled it with tea before offering it to me.

I said no thanks and went off to see if Henri Lemaire was at home.

And walked smack into Sarah Byrne.

7

OUTSIDE THE BOOKSHOP evening had turned into night, bringing a cold breeze into the city. A fuel barge glided past on the dark river. Its lights were diffused by mists that rose off the surface and drifted upward among the spires and gargoyles of Notre Dame.

My Renault 5 was around the corner in Rue Saint Jacques. There was a two-hundred-franc ticket tucked under the windshield wiper. No surprise. I had left the car on the sidewalk. All the legitimate parking spaces had been taken for blocks around when I'd arrived. I stuck the ticket in the glove compartment to be added onto the expense sheet the Byrnes would get when the job was done.

Taking off my jacket, I got the sweater from the back seat, shivering from the night chill until I had both of them back on. I drove to the Pont St. Michel and crossed over the Ile de la Cité under the floodlit Gothic grandeur of the Conciergerie, where Marie Antoinette had waited with thousands of others for her turn under the guillotine. In those days of revolutionary fervor the public executioner had been jubilantly called "Monsieur de Paris." Until he suffered the same fate when the fervor reached its crescendo.

On the other side of the Seine the traffic at that hour approached a crescendo of its own. Among the Châtelet's concentration of theaters and restaurants every intersection was snarled. There was no place left to park even on the sidewalks. I dived beneath the street into a big underground garage hacked out of what had once been an ancient burial ground filled with centuries of corpses.

I rode back up to the surface on an escalator, accompanied by a dozen cheerful prostitutes arriving to take over the neighborhood's night shift. We emerged near the sixteenth-century Fountain of the Innocents, surrounded by sex shops whose blazing neon signs overpowered everything else in sight. The whores clattered off to take their stations in doorways along the Rue Saint Denis. I walked two blocks in the other direction.

That brought me to the flamboyant modernism of the Centre Pompidou: vast expanses of glass held together by bands of thick pipes painted in circus colors. To me it looked like an oil refinery. But its museum and the view of Paris from the top have made it the most potent attraction in the city. Every day it draws more people than the Louvre and the Eiffel Tower combined. The big, open slope out front is a day-and-night carnival, with crowds forming circles around its street performers: jugglers, acrobats, quick-sketch artists, musicians, dancers, sword swallowers, fire eaters, escape artists, fortune tellers.

The biggest crowd this night was gathered around a one-man band who sang off-key while banging away at a Rube Goldberg contraption made of garbage can lids, bottles, bananas, and old hats. His own astonished chagrin at his failure to produce anything recognizable as music from the combination was getting him shouts of laughter and showers of coins as I crossed the slope in search of Henri Lemaire's apartment.

On the other side of the cultural center were several blocks of solid old buildings that were on the verge of becoming slums before they were renovated into pricey condominiums. The address Enid Jael had given me was inside one of those blocks.

It was a neatly maintained courtyard, lighted by an old-fashioned repainted lamppost set in the middle and flanked by small trees in concrete tubs. There were three entrances to the buildings surrounding the court. I started checking the names listed at the entrance to my left. No Henri Lemaire.

I was turning away to check the other two entrances when a girl came out of the middle one. She wore baggy trousers and the kind of leather jacket you have to pay extra for because the factory pre-ages it to look like something a hobo has thrown away after a decade of hard use. She was lugging two suitcases and heading past me toward the courtyard exit.

Her face hadn't changed much since the picture had been taken.

I said, "Sarah?"

She stopped and turned, startled. "Who are you?"

"Your parents are worried about you," I told her gently. I drifted toward her slowly, not wanting to scare her into dropping the suitcases and running. "They asked me to find you."

She didn't run. All she did was stand there with the suitcases growing heavier in her hands, looking annoyed rather than scared.

"So *you're* the one," she said. "Well, go tell Mommy and Daddy I'm fine and not to worry. Okay?"

"The thing is, Sarah, they're coming to Paris soon." I was close enough by then to grab her if she did try to bolt. "They'd like to see you."

Sarah Byrne made an exasperated face. "Not this time.

I've got to do my own thing for a while. Like we agreed before I came over. Tell them I'll see them some other time. Maybe back in California. And to please stop worrying about me all the time. I'm not a child anymore.''

"Do you know what your friends used your apartment for this morning?" I asked her.

"What are you talking about?"

Either she was genuinely puzzled or that acting ambition her father had mentioned was justified.

"If you don't know," I told her, "you'll be in danger once you find out."

She looked over my shoulder and repeated her question. "What is he talking about, Henri?"

I did a fast spin.

The young guy who'd just come out of the same entrance was tall, wearing a black corduroy jacket and black jeans that had been tailored for his wide-shouldered, slim-hipped figure. He had a face worthy of the movies: solid jaw and strong, sensual mouth, neatly chiseled nose, and big blue eyes, a mop of curly blond hair.

Like Sarah, he was carrying two suitcases. Unlike her, he didn't stand there letting them weigh down his arms. He threw them at me. While I was dodging them he leaped forward and launched a karate chop at the side of my neck.

But karate is like boxing: lessons don't help much unless you have reflexes that can be trained to deliver a blow with enough speed, force, and accuracy. Henri Lemaire was a shade too low on speed. I sidestepped the blow, caught his forearm with both hands as it went past, and yanked, using his own momentum against him.

He stumbled forward, off-balance, and I continued the pull, turning in a tight circle and swinging him around me. I slammed him against the wall beside the middle entrance, knocking the air out of him. He made a gasping noise and slid down the wall to his knees. I let go of his arm and got a grip on his jacket lapels, starting to drag him back up.

Then I heard the scrape of shoe leather on the flagstones behind me. I let go of him and executed a fast, dodging turn. Not fast enough. Something hard struck the side of my head. My being in motion in that instant saved me from getting hit squarely, but I got enough to send my brain into a spin. The rest of me spun with it, like a top wobbling to a falling stop.

I managed to break the fall with my hands before my arms went entirely limp. Then I was rolling over on the flagstones, sprawling out on my back. My brain stopped spinning, leaving one side of my head numb and the rest of it throbbing. I've been hurt worse; but having the experience doesn't make any repetition of it less unpleasant. I slitted my eyes open—just enough to see but not enough to advertise that I was still conscious.

From my ant's point of view she looked even taller than I remembered, towering over me. She was still dressed as she'd been that morning, but without the motorcycle helmet. Like Yuri had said: long black hair, long sharp nose. Plus hard cheekbones and chin, a very long, thin mouth, and small, dark eyes like black olives. Not a beauty, but striking as hell: not somebody other people would ignore. She was in her late thirties.

What she had hit me with was a short-barreled revolver. She now held it against her long, lean thigh, where it wouldn't be noticed by anyone looking down into the court from any of the apartment windows. It pointed at my stomach, ready to shoot if I made it necessary, and it looked like a .38. At that range it could tear through my guts and break my spine. I continued to play unconscious.

Sarah Byrnes had finally dropped her suitcases. She was helping Henri Lemaire to his feet. His nose and lips were bleeding. He shoved her away roughly, glaring at me and reaching for something under his jacket.

"Stop it," the tall woman told him. "We can't get the car out of this neighborhood fast enough if your neighbors call the cops."

It was said quietly, but with crisp authority. She sounded like a schoolteacher who was used to exercising control over unruly students.

Henri Lemaire obeyed her, slowing bringing his hand back into sight with nothing in it. Then he got out a handkerchief and wiped at the blood from his face, still glowering at me but under control.

"Get your bags and let's go," the tall woman told him and Sarah—and she kicked me in the head.

I rolled with it, but not far enough. Her reflexes were quicker than Lemaire's, and her boot was hard and heavy.

Later, when I checked my watch, I calculated that I'd been unconscious for no longer than three or four minutes. But it took longer than that to come all the way out of it.

" . . . drunk," a woman's indignant voice said.

My grandmother was bawling out my grandfather again, back in Chicago. He had been a captain with the police department there when he'd hit mandatory retirement age. After that he'd begun drinking more than was good for him.

" . . . take a lot more'n I've had to make me drunk," he told her heavily. "All I did was trip over the rug. Doesn't mean I'm drunk."

"Fine example you're setting for Petey."

"Don't worry about Petey. He's not some impressionable kid anymore. He's a man now—and a cop." He said that proudly. It was my grandfather's pride in his profession that had made me join the force, starting as an undercover narc, posing as a criminal from France hiding out in Chicago.

"Perhaps he is not drunk," a man said. "He could be sick, or . . ."

The woman made an angry sound. "Of course he's drunk. They are always coming into these courtyards to sleep it off."

They couldn't be my paternal grandparents. First of all, they were speaking in French, though it had taken me a while to realize that. Secondly, I began to remember that I was in present-day Paris, not in Chicago more than a decade ago.

I got my eyes partly open. The couple looking down at me were middle-aged, dressed in evening clothes.

"Well," said the man, "he's not doing any harm here. And if we don't leave now we'll be late."

"I still think we should call the police." But she took his arm and they turned their backs on me, hurrying out of the court.

It took me some time to get to my feet, more time to get to the nearest bar. I slumped into a booth and ordered black coffee, four aspirins, and Martell VSOP. I poured the cognac in the coffee and used it to wash the aspirins down. Then I waited for the mixture to do something about the condition of my head.

While I waited I tried to help the cure along by concentrating on other problems. I rejected the notion of breaking into Lemaire's apartment for a look around. Expensive new condos would be equipped with good locks, more than one. I didn't think I was up to that kind of job, not that night.

Besides, it was unlikely they'd left anything behind that would give me or the police any useful leads. They had been moving out for a reason, and the reason was probably that they'd been worried about being found. If what had worried them was the possibility that a police check of the late Fernand Claudel would lead to them, they would have moved away much earlier that day—as soon as possible after leaving his body behind at the Rue des Rosiers.

"So you're the one." That's what Sarah had said. I was the one that worried them, and they hadn't learned about me until late in the day.

How many people knew I was searching for Sarah Byrne? Too many. Little Yuri and the police, and a lot of others around the Rue des Rosiers. More around the Hotel Paradis, the American Church, and Shakespeare & Company. Mr. and Mrs. Byrne and their Paris attorney. I gave up on it and went on to the next problem.

Did Sarah know what they would use her sublet apartment for? Lemaire could have borrowed her keys without telling her the details. He also could have taken them from her bag without her knowing, after she'd moved into his apartment.

She hadn't *acted* as if she knew. But if she didn't, she was bound to find out—unless they kept her away from newspapers, radio, and TV. How would she react when she found out? Why would they want her with them, if they couldn't count on her cooperation?

Too many unanswerable questions for a sore brain. I wanted the police to catch the ones responsible for shooting up Fischman's Café. But unless and until I was sure Sarah Byrne was in it with them, my job still required that I try to get her to safety.

I ordered another cognac. It helped. My headache was

pulsing painfully but was no longer incapacitating. Leaving the bar, I went back to the big square in front of the Centre Pompidou.

The fortune tellers were all at one end—palm readers, astrologers, tarot readers. Each had the same basic setup: folding table and two chairs. I showed Sarah's picture to four of them before hitting one who recognized her. She was a fat, motherly type who said her professional name was Madame Nota. I sat down across the table from her and placed a hundred-franc note beside her tarot deck.

"She consulted me twice this week. The first time alone. The second time with a young man."

When I described Henri Lemaire she nodded. "Yes, he was the one." I tried a description of the tall woman who had clobbered me, but it didn't mean anything to Madame Nota. I asked what Sarah had consulted her about.

"It was difficult to be certain. She is a shy girl, reticent. And she admitted that she is not sure she believes in tarot divination." Madame Nota smiled. "I told her that sometimes *I* am not sure, either. But one has to believe in something, doesn't one? And I pointed out that faith is the greatest source of strength. After that the girl relaxed a bit with me.

"Her first concern was that she is obviously deeply infatuated with that young man and worried about whether he truly cares for her. She was also troubled about some enterprise in which her lover is involved and in which he wants to involve her. She is excited about it but frightened by it at the same time."

"What sort of enterprise?"

Madame Nota spread her surprisingly slender, graceful hands: a gesture of apologetic ignorance. "She did not say."

"Why was she frightened of it?"

"That, too, she would not explain, except to say it was very secret. And possibly dangerous. I asked if that meant it was something criminal, since she was so nervous about it. She laughed and assured me it wasn't. But I am not sure I believe her answer."

Madame Nota picked up her tarot cards and began shuffling them with smooth expertise. "The first time the girl came to see me, alone, the cards I turned up for her were the Sun, the World, the Lovers, and the Wheel of Fortune. I explained that the last could mean that the enterprise in which her lover was engaged *could* lead to great difficulties. And the card of the Lovers indicated that her young man was still undecided between her and another woman— or perhaps many others. On the other hand, the first two cards were entirely beneficent for her personally. Assurance that she will eventually achieve what she truly desires in life."

I watched her square the pack and put it down on top of my hundred-franc note. She still hadn't touched the money with her hands.

"The second time this girl came she was with her man. It was apparent that he was merely humoring her in agreeing to come. He sneered at me the whole time and asked me nothing. Most unpleasant. It pleased me when the first two cards I turned up for him were the Devil and Death. I wasn't cheating; they just turned up that way." Madame Nota grinned. "I gave him the worst possible interpretation of *that* combination. He didn't like that. He took the girl and went away before I could continue."

I questioned her further, but she had nothing to add. I thanked her and put another hundred francs on her table.

At the current rate of exchange, two hundred would only set the Byrnes back thirty dollars.

Madame Nota gave me her tarot pack. "Cut it three times and put it back together whatever way you wish."

I did so. She turned up the top card for me.

It was the Fool. He was striding ahead, blissfully unaware that a fox was about to take a bite out of him from the rear—and that his next careless step would be off the brink of a high cliff.

Swell. I decided to take my headache back to my apartment, feed it some codeine, and get a night's sleep before going all the way over that cliff.

8

THE EARLY-MORNING sky was a lovely translucent blue without a single cloud. But the sun was still low and the courtyard outside my apartment was still in shadow, preserving the night's cold like a sealed refrigerator. I walked the half block to breakfast wearing a cloth cap, a turtleneck sweater under my jacket, and a wool scarf over it. "Dress like an onion," French mothers teach their kids: with layers that can be peeled off and put back on, to outwit the vagaries of any day's temperature shifts. Most of the year it is excellent advice.

By night half of Paris seems to converge on the inexpensive restaurants around Place Contrescarpe. But by day it returns to being the heart of the Mouff, a neighborhood in the old meaning of the word, home to a manageable number of people of diverse incomes and ages who all know one another. Of the four bistros on the *place*, La Chope is the most popular much of the day, because it's on the side that gets the sunlight first. At one of its sidewalk tables a local dentist and a woman who taught at the nursery school a block away were flirting over their wake-up coffees before going to work. At another a couple of truck drivers who worked nights were sharing a bottle of red before going home to sleep.

I exchanged good mornings with them and went inside to order.

At the bar the Jewish baker and the Lebanese lawyer

61

were already into their daily argument about Mideast politics. At one end three university students were grouped around a table under the 1890s wall mosaic of the goddess of spring, cramming for their exams. At the other end a girl of eighteen named Claire sat in her habitual dim corner beside the pinball machines, sipping her habitual morning beer, her eyes vague and her face puffy. Both parents were alcoholics and she'd been born with it in her blood.

Georges, the Corsican waiter, started to work the espresso machine when he saw me. "The usual?"

I nodded and went out to one of the sun-warmed tables. Marie-Louise, a cabdriver who lived around the corner, brought her taxi to a stop in front of me, blew me a sleepy kiss, and yelled, "Two croissants, Georges!"

He came out with his tray and gave them to her. She stuck one in a corner of her mouth like a cigar, gave the other to the German shepherd sitting tall on seat beside her, and drove off.

Georges set my breakfast on the table: a big cup of café au lait and a generous slice of *tarte aux pommes*. He looked at the bruise on one side of my forehead. "Who hit you?"

"A lady."

"That's what happens when men treat women with too much respect. They don't treat you with any. Remember what Nietzsche said: If you go to a woman, take a stick."

"Next time."

Georges went back inside with his tray. I took off my scarf and started on my breakfast. The sun got higher and warmer. After the last bit of *tarte* I took off my cap. I finished the coffee, unbuttoned my jacket, and considered having a short *café noir* before starting out. A black Citroën with a uniformed police driver turned into place Contrescarpe.

It bumped its way up onto the raised pedestrian zone that takes up most of the center, narrowly missing three *clochards* who were sleeping under one of the four skinny trees. In the States a *clochard* would be called a skid-row bum. In France it's considered a philosophical way of life, a protest against the crass commercialism that insists people must work for a living.

Commissaire Gojon got out of the Citroën. One of the *clochards*, an elderly fellow named Max, sat up on the ground and cursed him loudly and at length. Ignoring the tirade, Gojon walked to my table. He smiled down at me—the sort of smile that cops know makes people nervous.

"You must not lie to me," he said with a gentleness calculated to do the same as the unnerving smile.

"No," I agreed.

"But you did."

"Recently?"

Gojon called inside for an *express* and a croissant. He sat down and regarded me in silence for a moment. Sunlight reflected in the lenses of his black-framed glasses, making it difficult to see his eyes. "You had a description of one of the terrorists and didn't tell me."

"That's not a lie. Yuri's the one who saw her face. I didn't. I assumed he'd tell you, if he trusts you. Since you know, I guess he does. Been able to identify her?"

"So far, no. Last night Yuri Suchar went through all of our photographs of known female terrorists, but there was nothing on this woman. Nor, Suchar assures me, is she in any Israeli files."

Max had crawled between the other two *clochards* and picked up a wine bottle. It was empty. He heaved to his feet and came toward La Chope to take up a collection for a full bottle. In his condition it wasn't an easy trek. That section of Paris was built on hilly country. The *place* tilts. Max had to tilt the other way to keep his balance. He made it to our table and stuck a grimy paw under my nose. "Save an old man from thirsty death?"

"Are you crazy?" I growled at him. "I *live* around here."

Max leaned closer, squinting at me. "Oh, excuse me. I must still be drunk." He turned on Gojon: "*You* don't live around here."

Gojon said mildly, "You know better than to try cadging money from police officers."

For a moment Max looked confused. Then he said, "Sure, I forgot you're the rotten chicken that got out of the cop car." He stood a little straighter and said, with dignity, "I spit on cops."

"All right."

"You know something? *I* used to be one. A chief inspector in the Police Judiciaire."

"Yes," Gojon said. "I know."

"It is a dirty profession," Max told him sadly. He raised one hand and made a sign in front of Gojon, like a priest giving what solace he could to a lost soul, and wandered off in search of tourists.

"Is that true?" I asked Gojon. "About Max being a chief inspector?"

"Yes," he said shortly. And then, eager to put that subject behind him: "What happened to your head?"

"I fell. Any leads through the dead man, Fernand Claudel?"

"We're questioning his friends, checking his recent movements. . . ."

Georges brought out Gojon's croissant and tiny cup of strong black coffee. Gojon undressed two sugars and inserted them in his cup, taking care not to make a splash. He stirred the dissolving cubes with equal care. "Have you found Sarah Byrne?"

"I haven't gotten my hands on her yet. I'm still looking."

Gojon picked up his croissant with a thumb and and two fingertips and dunked it delicately into his *express*. "Your Sarah Byrne was associated with political fanatics in America, the FBI informs me. But you knew that, of course."

I looked him in the eyes and said, "No, I didn't. Not when I saw you yesterday."

He bit off the soggy third of his croissant and chewed thoroughly before swallowing. "You do understand that I represent the authorities, and that it is unwise to withhold information from me."

"Absolutely."

Gojon dunked again and ate another third of his croissant. "You have an unfortunate record of disrespect toward authority. You lost two excellent positions because of it. First the one as a federal narcotics agent. Then your job as investigator for your Senate's Foreign Relations Committee here in Europe."

"There were some things, in both cases, that I just couldn't go along with."

"In that second case you almost went to prison for concealing evidence against a criminal suspected of acting as a broker in dealings between French and American firms."

The criminal he referred to was one of the biggest gangsters in France. He was also the man who had hidden my mother from the Gestapo in Marseilles during the war and then smuggled her out to Spain. I said, "The charge against me was dropped."

Gojon nodded blandly. "Because you blackmailed one

of your senators with some information about his personal life, as I understand. That will not work with me. I want to be sure you realize that. If you don't act with proper respect toward *my* authority, your mother's friends won't be able to save you.''

I watched him dunk and finish off his last piece of croissant and dust the crumbs from his fingertips. I asked him politely, ''Do you have the feeling I've been treating you without respect in some way?''

''Oh, yes. For example, that remark about *if* Yuri Suchar trusted me. What was that supposed to mean?''

''Come off it, Commissaire; you know the answer. Your Interior Minister himself has admitted that at least thirty members of the police, high and low, are also members of neo-Nazi groups. And that's a low estimate.''

Gojon's face darkened. It could have been anger or embarrassment. Or both. ''If you think that I am one of *those* . . .''

''I couldn't be sure yesterday. But if Yuri trusts you, I guess you're not. His sources of information in that area go deeper than mine.''

''Be careful, Sawyer. You don't want me for an enemy. Be very careful.''

''Yes, sir.''

He sighed, picked up his cup, and then looked at it in surprise. It was empty. The croissant had absorbed all the coffee. Gojon put the cup down. ''In any case, only thirty Nazis, among thousands of police. That is a healthy percentage.''

''During the war that tiny percent swung all the weight.''

''Only as long as the German Occupation lasted. And that won't happen again.''

''One can hope not.''

"You seem very sure the attack yesterday was the work of some group of the far right. *Why* are you so sure?"

I said carefully, "It's the logical thing to assume."

"Assuming and knowing are not the same. So far we've gotten eleven phone calls from people claiming to represent groups responsible for the attack. Terrorists of the left as well as the right. Including one I never heard of. The United European Brigade. Does that mean anything to you?"

It didn't. Gojon shrugged. "New ones spring up every year."

I got out a slip of paper on which I'd jotted down a Paris-issued motorcycle license number. "Just to prove I *do* want to cooperate with you, Commissaire—this *could* belong to one of the motorcycles used in the getaway after the attack yesterday."

Gojon scowled at the number, at me. "Where did you get this?"

I'd gotten it by phoning a contact in vehicle control before coming to breakfast and asking what license plate had been issued for a motorcycle belonging to Henri Lemaire. But what I said was: "A rumor that came my way. Could be wrong."

He continued to scowl but put the slip in his pocket and changed the subject: "One thing still intrigues me, Sawyer. That implication that you wouldn't trust me until Yuri Suchar did."

"It wasn't meant as disrespect. . . ."

Gojon ignored that. "It implies that you trust him a great deal."

"I trust him with *some* things. In *this* case. I wouldn't trust him with information about any of my Arab contacts. Any more than I'd trust them with information about him."

"You have such contacts, then," Gojon said blandly.

"You know I do."

"Yes." He took out a snapshot-size photograph and put it on the table between us. The man Yuri had killed at the Rue des Rosiers looked up at me from it. "According to one rumor, Fernand Claudel had contacts with certain Arab agents, probably Libyan, while a member of FANE. And continued to have them after he switched . . . to whatever group he did switch to."

"Wouldn't be too surprising. Qaddafi supports almost any group that makes trouble in any non-Moslem country. Right, left, or anything else, as long as they do make trouble."

"Yes. As in Ireland, where Qaddafi gives help to Catholic killers and Protestant killers impartially." Gojon pushed the photo across the table to me. "See what you can turn up about Fernand Claudel's recent associations among your Arab friends. The ones you won't tell Suchar about—or me. That would make me feel better about you than I do at the moment."

9

YOU LEAVE PARIS and enter North Africa when you go into the Barbes-Rochechouart district. It stretches between Pigalle and the city's main canal system, and most guidebooks don't mention it. The crowds in its streets are Algerian, Tunisian, Moroccan, a lot of them wearing the hooded cloaks of the Sahara and their native casbahs. Women's faces tend to be veiled or tattooed. But there aren't many women. The men outnumber them forty to one. Most of these men come to France alone to earn money for the families they left behind. They live six to a small room, sleeping in shifts, and save most of what their menial jobs pay so they can take it with them when they return home.

There are few non-Arabs in sight there except for the cops. Uniformed *flics* from the Police Nationale patrol the crooked little side streets in groups of four. Men of the C.R.S., the equivalent of American SWAT teams, sit inside their little buses, reading comic books with their riot guns close at hand while they wait for trouble.

It is a district where trouble is always seething below the surface, building pressure for the next eruption. There are just too many men cramped together in too little space with too little diversion and too many enemy factions among them. Some of the enmity goes back to tribal feuds in North Africa. The rest is divided among rival criminal mobs fighting for control of the area and political factions competing for the loyalty and donations of the inhabitants.

The main boulevard is under the Métro's elevated train tracks. A car can't move fast there. Too many pedestrians overflow into the street, detouring around sidewalks jammed with shoppers and strollers. I parked up on one of the traffic islands between two of the bulky piers supporting the tracks above.

Getting out, I chose the toughest-looking street vendor in sight and slipped him fifty francs to see to it that all of my car was still there when I got back. It required some slow-going footwork to maneuver through the crowds and get off the boulevard into a narrow side street. I followed it into a tangle of inner streets crossing one another at quirky angles. When I reached a corner café called the White Crow I sat down at one of the two outdoor tables and ordered a mint tea.

That far in from the boulevard I was extra-conspicuous among the solidly Arab populace. That was all right. The people there would figure I was one of two things. I could be a decently dressed tourist who'd gotten lost, in which case I should be treated with traditional Arabic hospitality. Or I was a plainclothes police detective and should be ignored.

Two of the other corners at that crooked intersection were occupied by a Moslem bookshop and a store displaying the items that sold best in this neighborhood: watches, portable radios and cassette players, suitcases and trunks. The house on the fourth corner, diagonally across from me, had a big sign over its arched stone entranceway: HAMMAN-DOUCHE. It was one of the places the men of the district went to shower, steam, and gossip. Few of their rooming houses had bathing facilities.

I sipped my tea. Very hot and very sweet. After a few

minutes the owner of the hamman came out and strolled across to me.

He was a tall Moroccan, thin except for the bulge of his paunch. His name was Mussa ben Zaer. It was thirty years since he had first arrived in France. He'd done well for himself in those years. He owned the White Crow as well as the Hamman, and also several of the neighborhood houses that boarded Arab workers. Instead of returning to his native city of Fez, he'd finally brought much of his family up to Paris to join him.

Two years before, one of his sons had killed another teen-age delinquent in a fight between two gangs of dope dealers from North Africa. While the cops were fine-combing the district for the boy, I had slipped him south to Marseilles. The same gangster who had hidden my mother during the war smuggled him aboard a cargo ship bound for Morocco, where some of Mussa's relatives were still keeping the boy safe and teaching him to behave himself.

Mussa sat down beside me without a word and rested one bony hand on the table, his long fingers skillfully manipulating his string of prayer beads. A lot of the denizens of the quarter were watching us and pretending not to. Now that Mussa had joined me they had me pegged as a cop. It wouldn't hurt Mussa. Everybody knew that no merchant could stay in business anywhere in Paris if he refused to give the police at least lip-service cooperation. Nobody would suspect him of giving more than that. His reputation for discretion was firmly established. If it hadn't been, he wouldn't still be around. He'd have been dead long ago.

"The machine-gunning in the Rue des Rosiers yesterday," I said.

"No Arab group had anything to do with that," Mussa told me. He shook his head slowly, several times, so that everyone could see he was giving me a negative response to whatever I'd asked him.

"I'm glad to hear it, because I'm looking for the ones who did it."

Mussa shrugged his scrawny shoulders elaborately. "Since they are not Arabs, that does not disturb me. But why are you interested?"

"One thing at a time." I reached down into the side pocket of my jacket and pulled out two photos: Fernand Claudel and Sarah Byrne. I'd had copies made of both after parting from Gojon. I put both on the table and tapped the one of Claudel. "He was in on the shooting. Got killed trying to get away. The name is Fernand Claudel. He may have had connections with some Qaddafi agents here in Paris."

Mussa was not fond of Qaddafi's people. A couple of years before a hit squad had murdered two anti-Qaddafi Libyans in Paris who had been about to invest in one of Mussa's new business ventures. He studied the photo and shook his head. "I am not familiar with him."

"I'd appreciate your checking around and seeing if somebody else is," I told him. "The girl may have been with him at some time. She's the one I'm interested in. American girl, here in Paris somewhere. Her parents are paying me to find her."

Mussa looked at Sarah's picture. Another shaking of the head. "I've never seen her. But I will check on both."

This time I was the one who shrugged for everyone to see. I removed the pictures from the table to stick them back in my pocket. Once they were out of sight under the table, I put them on my thigh instead. "Call me if you find out anything."

Mussa shook his head several times again. The hand on

the table continued to work his prayer beads. The hand below the table took the photos from my thigh and did a disappearing act with them. He got up and gave me a mock salute before strolling away across the intersection and back into his hamman.

I finished my mint tea and walked off without paying for it as though I were still a real cop. My car was waiting where I'd left it, intact. The street vendor exchanged nods with me and I climbed in and drove down to the Seine. Following the river, I headed east out of Paris. I wanted to see what I could turn up around Henri Lemaire's family.

Once I'd swung onto the A4 I had a bit more than an hour of fast expressway to cover. That would land me in Reims, source of most of the best vintage bubbly produced in the province of Champagne: Pommery, Krug, Mumm, Taittinger, Piper-Heidsieck—and Lemaire.

◫ **10** ◫

ALONG THE VALLEY of the Marne after Château-Thierry I had to turn on my fog lights. The damp countryside was exhaling thickening mist that blocked out the sky. Under the mist, gently tilting vineyards took up more and more of the landscape on both sides of the A4. They looked depressingly bleak.

In April, vineyards that far north are dismal even on the sunniest days. Just fields of dirt with rows of thin stakes connected by black wires. Between stakes the brutally pruned base of each potential vine resembles nothing more promising than a twisted chunk of long-dead driftwood.

That early in the spring it's hard to envision what it will all look like after those gnarled roots have given birth to the vines. In two months you won't be able to see the ground for the lush foilage spreading to the horizons. By the end of June the endless green fields will be in glorious flower. And exactly one hundred days after the flowering the growers will be harvesting tons of ripened grapes and putting them through their presses in preparation for shipment of their juice to Reims and a few other centers to be transformed into champagne.

The fog started to lift as the expressway turned north across the low mountain that separates the Marne from the city of Reims. The lifting didn't bring sunshine. What it brought was a heavy cloud cover that began leaking rain as I entered Reims. I followed the signs to the House of Lemaire.

Champagne is unlike other wines and wine regions. The differences between brands don't originate with the grape growers. They result from the blending decisions of the various firms that turn out the end product. Most of the vineyards that supply the juice of the three authorized types of grapes—Chardonnay, Pinot Noir, and Meunier—are distinct from the famous houses that make champagne from that juice.

Lemaire was one of these champagne houses. I found it on the southwest side of the city, just off boulevard President Wilson. None of the people I wanted were there. Lunchtimes, I was informed, were traditionally shared by members of the family at the Lemaire château, some miles outside the city. That suited me better anyway. My own lunch could wait. I worked out my approach while I drove to the château through a thin, steady drizzle.

"You are *not* Paul Rochefort," Christine-Marie Lemaire said firmly. Her old eyes regarded me questioningly.

"I didn't say I was," I lied. "Your butler must have misunderstood. I said I *represent* Monsieur Rochefort, who asked me to convey his sincerest respects to you, Madame." The extremely formal French I found myself using felt just right in front of the matriarch of the Lemaire family. "He especially wished me to express his hope that you are in good health."

"How very kind of him." She inclined her head slightly, like a queen accepting a courtesy from a minor baron. Her white hair framed a pinched face that had known a lot of physical pain and learned to endure it without flinching. "You may inform him that my health is no worse or better

than it has been for the last six years. Ever since that fool
horse fell and broke my back.''

She patted the arms of her motorized wheelchair and
added, ''My own fault, of course. I should never have
forced him over a jump higher than he was qualified to
handle.''

I guessed that explained why the stable had been converted into a four-car garage. It was off to one side of the
main building, which looked Renaissance but had almost
certainly been built much later. Or rebuilt, perhaps several
times.

There aren't many genuinely old châteaus left in Champagne. It's too close to the German frontier. A lot of wars
have ground back and forth over this region. It was not
happenstance that Reims was the place where the docu-
ments of surrender were finally signed by the commanders
of Hitler's forces.

I'd been ushered to the rear of the Lemaire château, into
a sunroom that connected through an open arch with a
paneled dining room where two maids were clearing up
after lunch. The sunroom wasn't living up to its name that
dismal afternoon. A couple of antique lamps had been
switched on to compensate. Their translucent jade lamp
shades cast reddish stains across the embroidered Porthault
tablecloth, the monogrammed silverware, the Spode cups
and saucers on the round table in front of Madame Lemaire.

The table had been set for coffee for three, but Christine-
Marie Lemaire was the only one there when I'd entered.
She was still eyeing me uncertainly. ''I've only met Paul
Rochefort once, several years ago when we had a problem
with someone counterfeiting our labels. Our own attorney

asked for his help because Monsieur Rochefort has connections with a firm that deals with such problems.''

I nodded. "Meacham Services, Ltd."

"Ah, you know about that."

"Of course." My tone implied an intimacy with all of Rochefort's affairs. As a matter of fact, I knew about this one because Jasper Meacham had asked me to tackle that particular job. I'd been too busy at the time. Jasper had managed to find the counterfeiters in less than three weeks without any help. But my tone did the trick, dissolving any lingering doubt Madame Lemaire had about me.

"Won't you sit down, Monsieur . . . ?"

I told her my name and took the seat she'd indicated: one of three Chippendale ladder-backs grouped around the table with her wheelchair. That gave me a view, through rain-streaked sliding glass doors, of a low-walled garden. A couple of men in hooded yellow slickers and black rubber boots were at work there putting together a rose trellis. Beyond the garden stark brown vineyards spread away to thick-forested hills at the far end of the estate. In spite of their extensive acreage, I doubted that these vineyards furnished more than a very small share of what went into the Lemaire blends. The rest would come from the fifteen hundred independents that supplied all the Reims champagne firms.

Madame Lemaire called to one of the maids in the dining room: "Solange, would you please bring another setting and a fresh pot of coffee?"

"Please don't bother," I told her. "I don't wish to intrude on your privacy. It was *Monsieur* Lemaire I asked to see. His office was sure I would find him here."

"My son is taking a phone call in the library at the moment. Whatever Paul Rochefort sent you here for, you can discuss with me until he returns. I get more privacy than I care for. And though Jean-Louis does manage our company now, I did so for some years after my late husband passed on. Business matters are not a mystery to me.''

"I'm not here on business. I've simply come to collect Sarah Byrne and take her home to her parents. She *is* underage, you know.''

She looked puzzled. "I don't know anyone of that name. Why does—''

"Please, Madame Lemaire,'' I interrupted. "Her parents are extremely worried about Sarah. Especially her mother, who is not well.'' I put a photo of Sarah Byrne on the table in front of her. "Perhaps you were given a different name. I've every reason to believe she is here.''

She studied the photograph and shook her head. "Whatever your reasons for thinking so, I'm afraid you are mistaken. I don't know this girl.''

I gave her a troubled look. "Henri Lemaire does live here—or is *that* mistaken? Do I have the wrong Lemaires?''

"What has my grandson to do with this?''

"She's his girlfriend. Sarah has been living with him for some time.''

A young woman carrying a tan Burberry raincoat and matching rain hat had come into the sunroom while we were speaking.

Madame Lemaire introduced her as her granddaughter, Gabrielle.

I guessed her age at about twenty-four. She had pale gold hair and moody, dark brown eyes, and the cool, detached poise of someone accustomed to creating a distance between herself and other people. Her dark green jacket and skirt were of soft woven wool, beautifully tailored to follow the contours of her figure without advertising them.

Her grandmother asked her, "What is keeping your uncle so long?"

"He was still on the phone when I came down past the library." Gabrielle Lemaire's voice came as a surprise: a deep husky sound that spoke directly to my hormones. It was also a voice suggesting strong energies held under too tight a control.

She had entered the room as though merely intending to bid her grandmother good-bye. Instead, she sat down, placed her raincoat and hat neatly on her lap, and eyed me with a grave curiosity. I suddenly realized whom she reminded me of: the young Grace Kelly you see in old movies on television, back when she was doing her first roles. The same weird combination of thoroughbred self-assurance, guarded vulnerability, and ladylike sensuality.

Her grandmother showed her the photo of Sarah. "Have you ever met this girl, Gabrielle? Monsieur Sawyer tells me she is . . . a friend of Henri's."

"No." Gabrielle Lemaire looked up from the picture and her eyes met mine, giving my hormones another nudge. "I don't know Henri's friends. I see as little of him as possible."

"Don't say things like that," Madame Lemaire chided gently. "Henri *is* your cousin."

"My misfortune."

"*Gabrielle . . .*" Her grandmother sighed and turned back to me. "Henri hasn't paid us a visit here in well over a month. He lives in Paris these days. I could give you the phone number at his apartment there."

"I have it," I said. "I've tried his apartment, but nobody is ever there. One of his friends told me he was here. With Sarah Byrne.''

''I can't imagine why he thought so. I'd suggest you keep trying his apartment until you catch him in. As far as I'm aware, Henri *is* still in Paris.''

''No, he's not,'' a man's voice contradicted. He had just entered the room: a solidly built man in his mid-fifties, with the kind of heavy self-confidence in his manner that some people acquire when they become too accustomed to the obedience of underlings.

''I forgot to tell you, Maman,'' he apologized. ''Henri phoned last evening. He was about to board a plane to India.''

Madame Lemaire stared at him. ''What on earth for?''

He shrugged and sat down at the table. ''He felt restless. He wants to tour the Orient for a few months before coming back here to settle in and learn the business.''

''If he doesn't finally get around to *that* fairly soon, he'll never learn enough to take over as director when you've become too old for it.''

He laughed softly. ''That still gives him plenty of time, one hopes.''

Madame Lemaire remembered her manners and introduced us. Jean-Louis Lemaire's handshake was strong. His smile seemed friendly, but it didn't move the set of his blunt mustache or alter the alert expression of his eyes. ''And what is your interest in my son?''

Before I could answer, a maid came in carrying a tray with a silver coffee pot and an extra service for me. Madame Lemaire and her granddaughter refused more coffee. Jean-Louis had a refill, black. I took mine with cream and wished there was at least some pastry to go with it. I was getting hungry.

Gabrielle Lemaire was studying her uncle thoughtfully, eyes narrowed. So far he'd avoided meeting her eyes.

As the maid left I showed him the picture of Sarah Byrne and explained a bit. Jean-Louis glanced at it and shook his head. "I don't know her. My son changes girlfriends so often it would be difficult to keep track of them all, even if I cared to try." He gave me another of those practiced smiles. "He's in that stage of sowing some wild oats before settling down, as most boys his age do."

Studying him didn't net me much beyond a certainty that I was being lied to. I wondered what his niece was detecting behind his armor. "Sarah was living with your son in Paris," I said. "Maybe he took her with him to India."

"I'm certain he took no one. Henri specifically told me he wanted to go off by himself for a time."

"If he flew off last night he's in India by now. I could make an overseas call to check with him, if you know where he's staying."

"I've no idea," Jean-Louis Lemaire told me. "I am not even sure if he intended to stay there for a while or to make a connection with a plane for some other country further east."

"Maybe his mother would know?"

Jean-Louis said somberly, "My wife died a few years ago."

"I'm sorry to hear that."

Madame Lemaire said, "Perhaps *Robert* knows something about this Sarah Byrne. Robert," she explained to me, "is my other son. Gabrielle's father. He lives in Paris, too." She looked to her granddaughter. "Your father does occasionally see Henri, doesn't he?"

"He used to. I don't know if he still does."

Jean-Louis was frowning at his mother. "I didn't know that. I don't want the boy influenced by *him*."

Gabrielle Lemaire said harshly: "You'd rather he continued being like *you*."

He looked at her for the first time. "I certainly don't want my son to wind up like your father—a disreputable rake."

"Instead of a successful fascist, you mean?"

Before her uncle could respond to that, Madame Lemaire clapped her hands together sharply and snapped, "Stop it, both of you! This instant!"

They did stop it, though her son's face was red with fury. Her granddaughter pushed her chair back and stood up. "Time for me to get back to work."

"Please soften your tone, Gabrielle," Madame Lemaire said, firm but loving. "And it is ridiculous, the money you are wasting, always calling taxis to go back and forth. Wait and let Jean-Louis drive you back into town."

Her granddaughter said, "No." The one word, cold, hard, and final. As though to reassure her grandmother that it wasn't directed at her, she bent and kissed the old woman on both cheeks, patting her shoulder.

Then she straightened, gave me a brief, direct look, and left the room.

Madame Lemaire looked at me regretfully. "I'm sorry you had to be a witness to that little family squabble, Monsieur Sawyer."

"All families have them," I soothed her, and I finished my coffee.

"True. Gabrielle remains quite fond of her father—though he *is* a bit of an embarrassment, unfortunately."

"A bit?" Jean-Louis rasped. "Robert is good for nothing but squandering his income from the business in the most sordid ways he can think of.''

"Please, Jean-Louis—not in front of a guest."

He nodded and sighed. "Let that girl go on being fond of Robert, and she'll wind up being *like* him."

"I doubt it. I understand the people she works for are more than satisfied with the job she does for them."

That seemed to be a sore point with Jean-Louis Lemaire. "For *them*. Not for us."

"She'll come back, in time."

"If she's still alive by then." Jean-Louis turned to me suddenly. "My niece has a Lancia. Do you know why she has to use taxis instead?"

I poured myself some coffee while I waited for him to deluge me with more information that had nothing to do with his son, Henri.

"She crashed her car into a tree, spent three weeks in the hospital, *and* had her license suspended because of suicidal reckless driving."

Madame Lemaire said, "I think the experience has calmed her down. Personally, I was relieved when you didn't get your police friends to drop the charge, the way you did when they were going to take her driver's license away for all those speeding violations."

"She never thanked me for that. So this time she can do without my help. Let her learn that loyalty to one's own family is more important than attachments to—other people."

When I rose from the table and thanked them for their time, I still hadn't learned anything further concerning Henri Lemaire.

I left the room hoping I was right in thinking I'd find Gabrielle Lemaire waiting for me.

⊠ **11** ⊠

SHE WAS WAITING in the crumbling remnants of a small Romanesque chapel beside the driveway, quite close to the château but hidden from it in a beech grove.

All that was left of the chapel was a section of the nave wall and part of an oven-vault chancel. Gabrielle Lemaire stood in the shelter of the vault, wearing her raincoat and hat. When I stopped the car she dodged through the rain and slid in beside me. As I drove out of the trees and across the bare vineyards toward the forested hills on the limits of the estate I glanced at her coat and hat. The only rain spots on them had been acquired between the chapel and my car.

"How did you get from the house to there? A tunnel?"

"Yes. There are a lot of them under these grounds."

That wasn't strange. The subsurface of the entire province of Champagne—including under its cities—is honeycombed by deep man-made caves and interconnecting tunnels. Some date back two thousand years to the Romans, who created the first ones by digging out the chalky stone beneath the region's surface for building material. Those were extended for defense purposes during the wars of the Middle Ages. They were extended further over the last couple of centuries as storage galleries for the aging of the sparkling wine. That far beneath the ground there are no seasonal temperature changes to disturb the measured fermentation process during the two to five years required for the transmutation of the blended juices into champagne.

Gabrielle Lemaire gestured at the dense forest on our left as the drive curved between the hills. "There's a whole network of interlocking caves over there, under and around the ruins of a twelfth century fortress abandoned long ago. Nobody knows most of it. A lot of the entrances are overgrown. Henri and I used to explore them." She was silent for a moment. "When we were children. Before he changed." Another pause. "Or maybe he was always the way he is now, only I didn't realize it then."

"What way is that?"

"Vicious."

"You don't like his father much, either."

"*Hate* would be a better word for it," she said quietly.

"Why?"

She stared straight ahead through the rain. "They . . . disapproved of a boy I was in love with."

It seemed a slender thing to hang a lasting hate on, but she didn't explain further.

The drive reached the open gate at the edge of the Lemaire property. "Where to?" I asked her.

"I have to get back to work, in Reims."

I turned left onto the road, heading toward the city. She removed her rain hat and shook her head, the pale golden hair swirling around her face. She noticed the Monte Carlo Rally sticker on my dashboard and looked at me with new interest. "You do rally racing?"

"When I can make the time. Only that once with this car. I've got another down south that I've used in the Corsican and Alpine rallies."

"It must be exciting."

"It is."

"I've sometimes thought about tackling a rally myself. More and more women seem to be getting into them."

"And winning, some of them. My codriver in the Corsican Rally was a woman."

"Oh?" Gabrielle Lemaire turned in her seat and studied me. "Maybe I *will* give it a try, when I get my driver's license back. I enjoy fast cars."

"Endurance and a feel for what the route will allow are more important than speed in a rally. Take the Monte Carlo: up to a week of grinding around twisty, narrow mountain roads in all kinds of weather and surface conditions. The object for a private-entry competitor is to make it to the finish within a respectable time limit. You don't get to the finish at all if you've wrapped your car around a tree along the way because you've misjudged how fast you can safely take a tight bend."

I stopped myself and laughed. "Sorry. End of lecture."

"I suppose you had a reason for delivering it."

"Your uncle Jean-Louis thinks you're suicidal."

She took her time before replying to that one. "I may have been. But I spent a while in a hospital thinking about it. Thinking of how near I'd come to killing myself. I decided I want to go on living."

"Well, that's a good start for any rally driver." I was holding down my impatience, waiting for her to get back to the subject without prompting. It's always a good idea to give an informant time to get relaxed with you first. But Reims was getting closer.

She pointed at the Monte Carlo sticker. "People usually put mementos like this on the *outside* of their cars."

"Makes the car conspicuous. Not a good idea, in my business."

"Which is?"

"I'm a private investigator." Okay, she was relaxed enough and Reims was getting *too* close. "I got the distinct impression you had something to tell me. Was I wrong?"

"Henri is in trouble, isn't he?" The possibility obviously didn't displease her.

"You must have a reason for thinking he might be."

"Because you're searching for him. And because Jean-Louis lied to you. That was Henri who called him on the phone just now—and not from India. I eavesdropped at the library door a little. Jean-Louis was shouting at him to get away from Paris—and out of something he's gotten involved in. I've never heard him so openly worried about anything."

"Did you overhear anything specific about what Henri's gotten himself into?"

"No. Do *you* know?"

"I suppose you've heard what happened at the Rue des Rosiers yesterday."

"The attack on the Jewish restaurant? Of course. It was on the radio last evening, and all the papers carried it this morning. One of the attackers was killed. . . ."

"I think your cousin Henri was one of the others who got away. Would that surprise you?"

Gabrielle Lemaire said slowly, "It would fit with what I know of him."

"Mind explaining that?"

Instead she answered my question with one of her own. "The girl whose picture you showed us—was she involved, too?"

"I'll know that when I find her. Which depends on finding Henri, at this point. Your parents in Paris might be able to help me with that."

"My mother lives in Lyons, with the man she married

after divorcing my father. He lives alone—between mistresses.''

''Your uncle and grandmother don't approve of him.''

''I don't give a damn about Jean-Louis's opinions of anything.''

''But you do care about your grandmother.''

Gabrielle Lemaire shrugged ruefully. ''She just doesn't understand about my father. I'm the only one who realizes the depth of the shock that makes him treat life like a bad joke.''

Once more, I sensed no willingness to explain further. ''I'd like your father's address and phone number.''

''I can do better than that,'' she suggested after taking another short, appraising look at me. ''I'll be going to Paris this evening. I usually do on Fridays after work, and spend the weekends at the apartment I keep there. If you want to hang around until I get off work and drive me in, I'll introduce you to my father.''

''That would be a help.'' I had more to accomplish in Reims before that evening anyway.

''I don't know how much he can help you, even if he's seen Henri lately. Henri would never let my father know if he was mixed up in something like that.''

''Your father might know some of the people Henri's been associating with lately.''

We were entering the city. Gabrielle Lemaire gave me directions for getting to the place where she worked: Taittinger. As I headed across town toward it I said, ''Your uncle is furious about your having a job with a rival champagne firm.''

''I know. That pleases me immensely.''

''Your grandmother thinks you'll come back to the family firm eventually.''

"Not as long as Jean-Louis runs it. Never, if Henri takes over after him."

Prying information out of people by taking advantage of their family antagonisms is dirty work. But the fact that I never liked it didn't stop me from doing it.

"I could use a photograph of Henri. Fairly recent, if you can get one for me."

"I'll slip one out of my grandmother's album when I go home after work to pack my weekend bag." The idea didn't seem to offend her well-bred sensibilities. She even grinned for a moment: the closest to a real smile I'd seen on her so far. Helping a detective do his job excited her. A substitute for reckless driving, maybe.

I questioned her about her cousin's friends in Reims. She didn't know any by name. "I do know Henri goes to Les Tours when he's back here. That's a brasserie on place Drouet d'Erlon. A favorite with the town's more affluent young ultra-right political hoodlums."

"Your cousin being one of them."

"In good standing. Henri takes his political leanings from his father. Jean-Louis is the money man behind the local branch of the National Front Party."

The National Front is as far to the right as you can go and still be a legal political party in France. For some years it had been regarded as a handful of political crackpots. Lately, however, the National Front had begun attracting millions of voters by blaming all of France's economic woes on immigrant Arabs. That still didn't add up to a father who would be pleased to learn his only son had gotten himself involved with homicidal terrorists. If that was what Henri had phoned about, Jean-Louis had reason to be scared.

"What about Henri's female friends?" I asked.

"I don't know any of them, either."

I tried a description of the tall woman who had been at the Rue des Rosiers and later knocked me out in the courtyard of Henri's apartment building—and hit paydirt.

"That *sounds* like Angelina Reisler."

I took a deep breath, let it out slowly, and waited.

"She used to teach German at a school here where Henri and I were students. Her father was a German soldier during the Occupation, and after the war he came back and married Angelina's mother. Henri used to have a terrible crush on her when he was fifteen and sixteen. Then she married another teacher, Leon Doniol, and they moved away. I don't know where."

"So her name's now Angelina Doniol," I said, mostly to myself. "Does she have any family around here?"

"Her father got killed in a rock-climbing accident when she was about eleven. Her mother died of illness a few years ago. But there's Doniol's father. He runs a souvenir shop across from the cathedral. He must know where his son and daughter-in-law went."

So now I had three Reims leads: the hangout of Henri's friends, Angelina Doniol's father-in-law—and the one I hoped my mother would shortly give me by phone.

Gabrielle indicated a bistro we were passing: the Café du Palais. "We can meet there this evening. Say between seven and seven-thirty?"

"Fine." I dropped her off at the champagne house of Taittinger and drove back through the city to the Place Drouet d'Erlon, across from the train station.

The brasserie where Henri met his friends when he was in town was as good a place as any to catch up with my delayed lunch.

* * *

The entrance to Les Tours was under one of the sidewalk arcades flanking the long *place*. I went inside and took a booth in the restaurant section. The brasserie's interior was sleek modern: chrome and dark wood and black imitation leather under soft indirect lighting. I had it almost to myself at that hour. The normal lunchtime was finished and afternoon drinkers hadn't started arriving. The only other clients were a couple of women having salads and wine at another booth and a man taking a coffee at the bar on the other side of the room. All three were expensively dressed. It was that kind of brasserie.

The waiter who came to my booth wore a navy-blue jacket with brass buttons, tuxedo pants, and a ruffled red shirt with a maroon bow tie. I ordered a beef stew in wine sauce, with roast potatoes and mixed salad. While the cook prepared it I went to a phone booth in the back to call my mother in Paris. I had phoned her early that morning about what I needed.

Babette had it ready for me: "Patrick Bertrand. The director of production at Pommery. He's exactly what you asked for. A life-long resident of Reims; knows everybody. In the war he was the local Resistance leader. I got his name from a former Resistance doctor from that area who has since retired here in Paris."

"Did you ask him to phone Bertrand about me?"

"Of course. Don't worry. You'll get a friendly reception."

I was sure of it. Former Resistance members form one of the best old-boy networks in France. "Thank you, Babette."

"Don't forget you're taking me to the Elysée reception this Sunday. And *be sure* to wear a necktie. Not one of your usual sloppy scarves."

"They're not sloppy. Ties make me feel like I'm being strangled."

"Pierre-Ange!"

"Yes, ma'am . . . . Don't worry; I'll wear the tie."

After disconnecting, I looked up the Pommery number and phoned it. Patrick Bertrand's secretary took a few minutes to locate him and get him to the phone.

"I'm very busy until about five-thirty," he told me. "Can you be at my office at that time?"

"No trouble," I assured him. "I'll be there." Leaving the booth, I went to the end of the bar and paid the cashier what her phone-meter had clocked for my calls. Shortly after returning to my booth the waiter brought my meal.

"Has Henri Lemaire been in yet today?" I asked him.

"Haven't seen him around here for a long time."

I gave him a surprised frown. "Henri told me he'd be in Reims all of this week. He said this was the place to find him."

"He usually drops by when he's in town. But not this week. At least, not when I've been on duty."

My frown got worried. "Maybe some of his friends would know. Henri said this is where they hang out."

The waiter nodded. "Lunchtimes, and later in the day. None of them here right now."

"Well, thank you anyway. I'll probably come back later, if I don't find him on my own before then."

My meal rated a couple of stars: as delicious as it was substantial. Nothing but the best for the clients of Les Tours, obviously. The bill was nothing to sneeze at, either. I paid it with a credit card to leave myself enough cash to get me through the weekend.

The tip I left was lavish, to make sure the waiter would remember me kindly when I came back.

Outside it had stopped raining. But the clouds were, if anything, darker and lower, threatening an early dusk. The cathedral was only a few blocks away. I stuffed my cap in my pocket and walked it.

Most of Reims is fairly new, constructed after one or another of the two wars that leveled most of the buildings dating before this century. But the magnificent cathedral looming above the city's center is very old. This is where Jeanne d'Arc crowned Charles VII king of France. The bulk of it has been standing there for over seven hundred years.

Not all of it. Some parts were destroyed by shelling and fire in World War I. The twenty years of restoration work that followed couldn't replace all that was lost. What remains, however, is still one of the glories of Europe.

I had to cross the big square in front to reach the souvenier shop of Angelina Doniol's father-in-law. Midway, I stopped for a look at one of the tall statues under the deep arch of the cathedral's entrance.

It is the most famous stone angel in the world. They call it "The Smiling Angel." Its smile is as disturbingly ambiguous as that of the Mona Lisa. Experts like my mother have debated for centuries over whether it is a smile of comfort or of mocking indifference to humanity's fate.

The girl I'd had an affair with at the University of Chicago had once sent me a picture postcard of the Smiling Angel. She hadn't written anything on the back of it except an exclamation mark.

I stood there and took a long look at that stone statue and its smile. But if there was any resemblance between us, I still didn't see it. And at that point I was more interested in another "angel": Angelina Doniol.

⊠ 12 ⊠

SHE LOOKED AT me from the pages of the snapshot album. A bit younger-looking, but otherwise the same as when she had given me the headache the previous night. The striking, hard-boned face framed by long black hair now had a name: Angelina Doniol.

One shot was a closeup of her staring directly into the camera with an impatient smile. In another she was beside what looked like a public swimming pool, wearing a sensible one-piece bathing suit that she filled in spectacular fashion.

Max Doniol tapped a picture of her standing under a tree with a handsome young man a few inches taller than she, which made him about my height. "That's my son Leon."

"Good-looking man."

"Sure. Leon could have married almost any girl in town. Instead, he had to pick Angelina Reisler. Not that I can blame him. Angelina's not the prettiest, but she certainly is one hot piece of lively woman. No man she crooked a finger at ever said no; I can tell you that."

Max Doniol smiled nostalgically. "I have to admit, I sometimes felt pretty frisky around her myself, in spite of being her father-in-law. If Angelina had ever crooked a finger at *me* . . . Well, she didn't, so I never had to wrestle my conscience over that particular moral decision."

"You don't think your son would know where she is now?"

"He might, for all I know. Leon never talks about her when he comes to visit. Hurt pride, you understand."

"Why did she leave him?"

Max Doniol shrugged. "Some other man, I *think*."

He hadn't been in the shop when I got there. A saleswoman he'd left in charge had directed me to his upstairs apartment, where he'd gone to have a cup of tea. He was a scholarly-looking man in his late fifties, with an easy friendliness. A man who liked company. My story about trying to locate his daughter-in-law because of a small inheritance left by a distant uncle in Germany was accepted without suspicion. I found myself inside his apartment, declining a cup of tea, before he got around to explaining why he couldn't be of much help to me.

His son and daughter-in-law had left Reims for teaching jobs in Paris. But over three years ago Angelina had left Leon. Neither had bothered about a divorce, but Max Doniol was fairly sure his son hadn't seen her since.

I had then explained my other problem to him: "We're not absolutely certain your daughter-in-law is the correct Angelina Reisler. I had a picture of her to show you. But it was in my wallet, and a pickpocket apparently removed that sometime this morning in Paris."

His nod was all sympathy. "That happened to me last year. My money, identification papers, driving license, checkbook. All suddenly gone. It feels like being raped, doesn't it?"

"I'm afraid I'm the wrong gender to be able to answer that question. But there *is* the element of violence missing. I've never heard of a brutal pickpocket."

"Nevertheless, the feeling of being violated is definitely present—and very unpleasant." He'd finished the tea in his cup and added, "If you remember what the girl in your stolen picture looked like, I have some of Angelina I could show you.''

''I hoped you might. . . .''

So here we were, seated on Max Doniol's sofa together, with his album on the coffee table in front of us opened to the pictures of Angelina Doniol.

''Frankly,'' he admitted, ''I can understand Angelina walking out on Leon. My son is a nice, intelligent boy, but a bit of a stick-in-the-mud. And as I mentioned, Angelina is a lively woman. In body and mind. Full of electricity and ideas.''

''What sort of ideas?''

''Oh, about improving the world and people's lives. You know, the *big* problems young people still think you can do something about, if ordinary citizens band together and get active enough.''

''*Was* she active?''

''If you mean did she join any political groups, I don't think she ever got that far. She wanted to, but Leon was deadset against her doing it. So was I, to be honest, though I didn't say so. Angelina's a strong-minded girl. I didn't want her mad at me. But her opinions were much too left-wing for me, and I consider myself a liberal politically.''

''Left-wing . . .'' I repeated dully. It was unexpected.

''Extremely.''

It just didn't fit. I tried another tack: ''Her father was part of the Nazi occupation force here. How did she feel about the German part of her heritage?''

''She took pride in it. All the great German composers and artists and philosophers. That's why she studied the language and wound up teaching it. But she was disgusted about what the Nazis did.''

I was finding it difficult to get a handle on the people I

was hearing about. Henri Lemaire, who had an infatuation with the late Adolf Hitler but put a Che Guevara poster on his wall. Angelina Reisler Doniol, who was supposed to be anti-Nazi but took part in an anti-Semitic terrorist shooting. Took part, hell—from my brief but memorable acquaintance with her, I figured her as the *leader* of that terrorist group.

And what pulled a right-winger like Henri and a leftist like Angelina together? It had to be more than sex. Or maybe not; I'd learned long ago not to expect people to be consistent when their primary drives take over.

"Her father wasn't a Nazi, either," Max Doniol was saying. "He was what people around here called a good German. One of the Occupation soldiers who tried to make as little trouble for the local citizens as possible. Of course, he was Wehrmacht, not SS. I never met anybody who didn't detest those SS monsters. But Angelina's father—he was more than welcome when he came back here after the war. Everybody was sorry when he died."

I got Leon Doniol's Paris address and phone number from his father. Then I said, "If you don't mind, I *could* do with a cup of tea now."

"My pleasure. I'll brew myself another while I'm at it." He closed the album and went into his kitchen.

I reopened the album. When he returned it was shut and the closeup of Angelina was inside my pocket.

After leaving him I stopped in the cathedral square to look up again at the face of the stone angel. It looked back down at me with that creepy smile.

Sometimes you dig up what you're after as simply as that. Other times you hit surface rock before you get started, the way I did when I got back to Les Tours.

The sleek brasserie was filling up. My waiter did remember me kindly. He waved a hand when he saw me come in, and he turned to speak to two big-shouldered men in business suits having drinks at the bar. Just eager to be of help and too quick about it for me to stop him.

The men turned on their black-padded bar stools as I walked toward them. One was in his twenties and the other about ten years older. Both had wrestler's necks that bulged the collars of their silk shirts, and faces that stayed hard no matter what expression flickered across them. Their hands were heavy and scarred, with beautifully manicured nails buffed to a shiny polish. You saw the type around every political party: muscle to control its gatherings and intimidate those of its opponents.

The older one had a friendly smile in place when he was fully turned toward me. The other was still working at getting rid of a scowl as he sized me up.

The smiler said, "Michel tells us you're looking for Henri."

"That's right." Michel, the waiter, was still standing close, waiting. I gave him another tip and he went away. "I brought a message for Henri," I said. "He was supposed to be here but he's not. Do you know where I can get in touch with him?"

"My name's Meyssonier," the smiler told me. He jerked a thick thumb at his young friend: "This is Julien Dalmas." He waited, watching me.

"Marcel Royan," I said, trying to watch them both at the same time. "Maybe Henri has mentioned me to you."

The younger one's scowl came back. He tried to wipe it out with a toothy grin.

The older one's smile got even more friendly.

My nervous system went on full alert. They knew it was

the wrong name. That had to mean they had a description of me and the name that went with it. Jean-Louis had made some phone calls after I'd left the château.

"So what's the message?" the smiler asked me.

"It's for Henri alone," I said. "Nobody else." Just words, on both sides now. Until I got out of there or they managed to hang on to me. "So if you don't know where he is, just say so."

"Take it easy. We know, but . . ." He glanced around. "Let's get some privacy." When he slid off the bar stool, I saw that he was about an inch shorter than me. He draped a friendly left arm over my shoulders and confided softly, "There's a place out back where we can talk."

The scowler was taller than both of us when he was on his feet. He led the way toward the rear of the brasserie. The smiler steered me after him. I let myself be steered. There was no way of knowing how many of the other men in the place would jump in on their side if I made a problem right then and there.

We went past the phone booth and along a corridor past the kitchen. The scowler kept on ahead, his right hand in his jacket pocket, moving toward a door with a latch lock. Probably the door to a back alley or some dim little courtyard where the brasserie put its garbage.

My smiler still had his arm draped over my shoulders. His hand began to drift from my shoulder toward my neck.

I stamped my heel on his instep and rammed my elbow into him below the ribcage. He gasped and went sideways, bending over in pain. I locked my fists together and clubbed him across the hinge of his jaw.

The scowler spun around as his friend settled into an ungainly heap on the corridor floor between us. Brass knuckles glinted on his right fist.

"When you get close enough," I told him quietly, "the first thing I'm going to do is break your right elbow. Then I'm going to smash both your kneecaps."

He looked uncertainly from me to his unconscious partner and stayed where he was. Not a type who enjoyed suddenly finding himself on his own, even with the brass knuckles.

I started backing away. He squatted and shook his friend, probably trying to wake him up so he could ask his advice.

I turned and walked swiftly through the brasserie, out to where my car was parked under the trees in the middle of the *place*. While I unlocked it and got in I kept glancing back at Les Tours. When I got the motor started I looked again.

The scowler was standing under the arcade in front of the brasserie, peering in my direction and talking to himself. That didn't strike me as funny. It made me damned uneasy. My guess was he was memorizing the license number of my car.

A very good reason to get out of town without too much delay. But I had appointments to keep. First at Pommery, and later with Gabrielle Lemaire.

So I didn't leave. And I didn't stop feeling uneasy about what the town might have in store for me that evening.

⊠ **13** ⊠

"WE ARE ALWAYS scared," Patrick Bertrand said.

We were descending a series of dimly lighted stone stairways under the Pommery buildings. Like me, the company's production director was of mixed nationality: half French and half Irish—a distinguished gentleman with neatly barbered dark hair and a short white beard. He was talking about the need to be humble about one's abilities when making decisions during the development of a champagne.

"One must always remember that man's contribution enters the process as an uncertain third factor. God is the most important factor. Then the sun that ripens the grapes in the fields."

"And then the production director."

"Together with his team of specialists," Bertrand amended. "The scariest decision, of course, is the first one: the choice in blending wines from the different vineyards to achieve a perfect balance—the right harmony, you might say. The *blending*—that's where each champagne house creates its own style. It's like different orchestra conductors recording Beethoven's First Symphony. Each has the same score and the same musical instruments at his disposal. Yet no two get the same result."

I was used to wine makers waxing mystical about their craft. So I just nodded understandingly.

"And in the years that follow that first decision there are

so many others to be made," Bertrand went on, obviously more enthralled than worried. "We are constantly checking how a blend is coming along. Deciding if something further should be done to improve the ultimate result. There are no absolute rules that guarantee success, Monsieur Sawyer. It is very *sensual*, creating wine. We *taste* the blend, we *smell* it, we look at the color. We have to depend on our senses to make the choice."

"You can't have made too many wrong choices so far," I pointed out, "judging by your label's reputation."

Superstitiously, Bertrand stepped aside at the bottom of a flight of steps to rap his knuckles against an old wooden wine press. "*So far* . . . but we always have stage fright. A blend looked, smelled, and tasted marvelous the last time we checked—but will it continue to do so next month, next year? It's like having children. You're never sure how they will turn out, no matter how clever and careful you are in raising them."

"Or like a love affair," I suggested. "She was crazy about you last week. But will she still be the next time you meet?"

Bertrand's grin was surprisingly boyish. "Exactly. It is fatal to become too sure of yourself. In love, in raising children—and in creating champagne."

"And Jean-Louis Lemaire *is* too sure of himself?" It was my interest in Henri's father that had started Bertrand explaining the delicacy of decision-making in their business.

He pondered his reply as we entered a maze of wide, lofty tunnels thirty meters below ground. At that depth the temperature was exactly right for the bottles of aging champagne in the racks that filled much of the space in every tunnel and cave we passed through. These wine cellars,

Bertrand had told me, linked a hundred and twenty of the ancient Roman chalk pits and now extended some ten miles. They were stocked with twenty million filled bottles: enough to supply the firm's customers over the next four years. The electric lamps there were turned down to single-candle power: just enough to guide us through the vast maze, not enough to affect the continuing fermentation. With most of the workers gone upstairs to clock out for the day, the dim tunnels were so silent you could almost hear all that champagne quietly cooking away in those twenty million bottles around us.

"In my opinion," Bertrand told me finally, "Jean-Louis Lemaire does not give sufficient weight to the judgments of those who work for him. That, I think, is beginning to lower the quality of the Lemaire champagnes."

It wasn't the kind of information I was after, but I let him work his way toward what I did want in his own way.

"Here we believe very much in *team* work. We want the opinions of everybody in the house. From the experts in our laboratories to our secretaries and mailroom boys. At various stages all of them sample the blends and we ask their opinions. Naturally, there does have to be a final authority."

"And at Pommery, that's you."

"Yes. Ultimately, I'm responsible for each decision, no matter how many opinions I listen to. But I do take those other opinions into consideration. Jean-Louis Lemaire, it seems to me, is *so* authoritative that it makes others wary of saying anything that might contradict his own feelings."

"That's a common problem," I said, "with fascists."

Bertrand frowned uncomfortably. "I wouldn't call him a fascist, exactly . . ."

"What *would* you call him, politically?"

"He's certainly too extreme; that I have to admit." Bertrand was trying to pick his words carefully. "*I* am a political conservative. But his party's racial attitude is not something I would care to be associated with. Too reminiscent of Hitler. With the Nazis it was against Jews and Gypsies. With the National Front Party it is against all the Arab immigrants in France. And if they succeed with that, God knows which of us they'll turn on next."

"Gabrielle Lemaire just says her uncle is a fascist and lets it go at that."

"Ah, you've talked to *her*."

"Yes."

"Well, she has her own reason for disliking him. A very unpleasant story . . ." Bertrand grimaced. "What's wrong with her uncle goes back to his father. Not the best choice of someone to emulate. Jacques Baudou used to work for the father, so he can tell you more about that . . . *when* we find him."

He paused at a point where four of the underground galleries met and peered into each. They stretched far off through dimness into darkness without a soul in sight. Bertrand made up his mind and we turned into the one to the right.

"Jacques is usually around here at this time of day," Bertrand told me. "Making sure all the *remuage* has been attended to. But he may have already gone up to his office."

Jacques Baudou was Bertrand's *Chef du Caves*, in charge of all the men who worked in the cellars. The champagne in this section was all near the end of its aging process. The wine racks here were a sloping type called *pupitres*, holding the bottles with their necks tilted down. The *remuage* consists of giving each bottle a sharp twist every single day, to encourage the sediment to sift down against the temporary cork. After some six weeks of that they freeze the neck of the bottle and pop out the frozen sediment with the cork. This is followed by another of Bertrand's delicate decisions: how much of which wines to add to the bottle in order to make up for the disgorged sediment before the final corking, wiring, and labeling.

The man who supervised all this finally appeared when we entered the bottom of one of the Roman quarry pits. At its base the pit was wide, with a couple of big tunnels connecting to it. An anchored ladder ran up one side to a smaller tunnel about fifteen feet above our heads. Above that the sides of the pit tapered in sharply toward a narrow opening high above us at ground level, covered to keep out rain and daylight.

Jacques Baudou emerged from one of the bottom tunnels wearing shapeless dungarees and a woolly cardigan, spreading thick arms wide in an exaggerated display of relief: "I've been searching all over for you! Did you get lost in my world?"

He had a fringe of crisp gray curls around a bald pate that gave him the look of a monk. But his mobile face was that of a sad clown: the kind that masks shyness behind exuberance and sometimes exuberance behind shyness. He appraised me with mock severity while we were introduced. "Are you a man who knows good champagne when he tastes it?"

"I'm not an expert," I told him. "But I do enjoy drinking it when I get the chance."

"You'll get the chance. I told Agnes, my secretary, to leave a bottle for us in my office before she went home." He looked to Bertrand: "Well, Patrick, are you still spry enough to use the shortcut up the ladder, or are you getting too old for that?''

"I'm two years younger than you are, Jacques," Bertrand growled, "so don't be so damned impertinent." He shrugged at me. "I told you Lemaire exercises too much authority. Now you realize that I exert too little around here."

With that he scooted up the ladder and into the tunnel above us with the agility of a twelve-year-old. I went up after him, followed by Jacques Baudou, who turned out to be the slowest climber. The rough stone tunnel up there had only a few inches of clearance above my head, and it was so narrow that we had to go through it single file.

Baudou called past me to Bertrand: "Guess what Agnes has done—gotten herself pregnant."

"I noticed."

"Women! They make all of us men look like fools. *They* create *life*. Leaving us trying to make up for it with some other kind of creation: art, champagne, woodwork. Anything, just to prove to them that we're good for *something*."

At the end of the tunnel we entered a well-lighted office, still underground. There was an old-fashioned rolltop desk and a long mahogany table with swivel chairs around it, their leather padding considerably worn. An elegant silver ice bucket was waiting on the table, holding a chilled bottle of champagne. Beside it three antique tulip glasses rested on brown plastic coasters.

Jacques Baudou motioned for us to sit down. As he opened the bottle and poured I got a look at the medallion. It was the very best: a Brut Vintage, the result of an exceptionally good year and extra-long aging. Baudou handed me my glass first. Then he and Bertrand just sat and watched me expectantly—with a tinge of anxiety.

I took my time with the required ritual: studied the fine bubbles rising in the wine, smelled the aroma, then took a small sip and leaned back in my chair while I savored and thought about it. After a decent interval I delivered what they were waiting for.

"I'm still no expert, but I've never tasted anything better."

Their smiles of pleasure rewarded me. They raised their own glasses in a silent toast to my good judgment and we drank together. Jacques Baudou was refilling our glasses when Patrick Bertrand brought up the point of our meeting.

"I've already explained," he told Baudou, "that you know more about the Lemaires than most because you worked for their company."

Baudou nodded. "Before and during the war," he told me, and his pleasure in our sharing of his champagne was suddenly gone. "I probably wouldn't be alive except for that," he added darkly. "So I suppose I *ought* to be grateful about it. But I never was and never will be."

⊠ **14** ⊠

WHEN FRENCHMEN OLD enough to have been involved in it speak of the World War II, it is often with a disturbing mixture of embarrassment and anger. France lost far more men in World War I. But the later war divided the French people against one another in a moral civil war whose emotional scars have still not completely healed.

In those days, they told me, the head of the Lemaire family and its business was Emile Lemaire, Christine-Marie's husband, grandfather to both Henri and Gabrielle. And a prominent collaborator with the Nazi authorities during the war.

"For which they rewarded him handsomely," Patrick Bertrand said. "Emile Lemaire's company was helped to keep up full production, while all the others had to cut down drastically. He got the first choice of the best from every vineyard, leaving the rest of us to make do with whatever he didn't want. The others had their stocks looted. Not Emile Lemaire. And when they began taking workers away from the other companies and sending them to Germany as forced labor, they didn't take a single man away from Lemaire."

"Which is why *I* escaped becoming forced labor there," Jacques Baudou said heavily. "With my loose mouth I wouldn't have survived two weeks in Hitler's fatherland. But when it's a man like old Emile who's responsible for your survival, it shames you."

Bertrand reached over and punched his arm to break him out of it: "You always exaggerate, Jacques. You were able to help us in the Resistance often enough. With money, food, hiding places, information."

"It eased my conscience somewhat," Baudou granted.

Bertrand turned back to me. "The thing is, Emile Lemaire was worse than just a collaborator. He became the power behind the Vichy government in this area. And *he* was chiefly responsible for the instructions to the Vichy police here to do a thorough job in hunting out Jews for shipment to the German death camps."

Bertrand's tone had become very bitter. He was touching one of the most sensitive memories of the war: that of the French collaborators who had played their part in the extermination of whole Jewish families—from the babies to the grandparents—with much more enthusiasm than most of the Germans of the Occupation forces.

"Once the Nazis were defeated," he resumed, "there was a certain amount of both official and unofficial retaliation against certain collaborators, as I'm sure you know. The government never got around to considering how to punish Emile Lemaire. Perhaps it would have, in time. But less than two months after the war, one of the transported Jews came back here. One of the very few who did live to return. The man's wife, mother, and children were among those who did not.

"One morning when Emile Lemaire came into Reims this man was waiting for him and killed him. Four bullets in the face."

"Much too easy a death," Jacques Baudou grumbled.

Bertrand looked at him. "There's a place in hell for people like Emile Lemaire. I doubt it's an easy one."

I watched Baudou stop himself from slapping Bertrand's

faith down with a sarcastic rejoinder. He grimaced and said softly, "One can only hope you're right."

"What happened," I asked, "to the Jew who shot him?"

"He was arrested but never brought to trial. Feeling against collaborators still ran too high for that back then, and a lot of private scores were being settled. The man was finally released and he went away."

"The Lemaire business doesn't seem to have suffered from that reaction against collaborators."

Bertrand shrugged. "Emile's death let the government off the hook. They didn't *want* to hurt the Lemaire firm. It's too important to the country as a source of taxes and a place of employment for people in this area. Once his widow took over running it—well, no one had anything against *her*. Christine-Marie had no part in her husband's crimes. And she was never involved in politics. Not before the war, during it, or after."

Jacques Baudou was suddenly smiling again. "Of course not. Marie-Christine considers politics beneath her notice. Something too sordid for an aristocrat. And she *is* an aristocrat, in the true sense of the word. The only trouble with her was that she also adhered to the virtues of a traditional wife. Never considered openly opposing her husband. But on the sly she did sometimes go around him."

His smile broadened. " 'For the poor'—that's what she'd always say when she slipped me some extra money. But I'd swear she knew I was giving it to Patrick's Resistance group."

Bertrand was nodding in agreement. "A good woman. *And* she turned out to be an excellent manager of the Lemaire company. Right up to the time her son took over from her."

"That was the day," Baudou told me, "that I quit Lemaire and came to work here. One thing for sure, I wasn't going to work for *Jean-Louis*. I never did like him, even when he was a kid, during the war. Arrogant teenage brat. Strutting around trying to give orders. Trying to be like his rotten father. Well, he's getting closer to succeeding all the time."

"And he's never forgiven the world," Bertrand added, "for letting the man who killed his father go free."

"What about the other son?" I asked. "Jean-Louis's brother, Robert?"

"Robert's nothing like Jean-Louis," Jacques Baudou said. "He was a nice boy. A little weak, maybe, but with his heart in the right place. Ran away when the Nazis occupied France. He was about sixteen then, three years older than Jean-Louis. He got all the way to North Africa and joined a bunch of anti-Vichy French troops. Came back as part of the Liberation forces. Never knew anything about the monstrous things his father did until after old Emile got killed. Finding out hit him hard. I don't think he's ever gotten over it. He became ashamed to be among people who knew about it. Began spending most of his time in Paris."

"Since his wife left him," Bertrand said, "Robert never comes back here at all."

So that was the "shock" Gabrielle Lemaire had referred to in talking about her father to me. "According to his family," I said, "he leads a pretty dissolute life."

Jacques Baudou gave me an ironic smile. "They mean he avoids such *serious* interests as business and politics."

"Unlike his brother. I understand Jean-Louis is a local power with the National Front people."

"Uh-huh. With some of some of our cops and government functionaries in his pocket—along with every thug with neo-Nazi leanings.''

Bertrand said carefully, ''Jean-Louis also has a certain amount of influence in the national government. As you would expect, considering his wealth, family background, and many business associations.''

It was his way of warning me to be cautious about antagonizing Jean-Louis Lemaire.

About Jean-Louis's son, Henri, neither of them had much in the way of new information for me, other than the fact that in the past Henri had helped his father organize National Front meetings and get out the vote for that party at election times.

''He still comes back from Paris sometimes,'' Bertrand told me, ''to help their regional candidates with their campaigning.''

''According to his father,'' I said, ''Henri's only in Paris to sow some wild oats before settling down to learn the business.''

''Jean-Louis does expect his son to inherit his position eventually; that's certain. And he's more indulgent with Henri than he'd be with anyone else.''

''He *dotes* on that boy,'' Jacques Baudou said. ''Like he did with his father. In my opinion, Henri is the only person in the world Jean-Louis has any human feelings for.''

About Gabrielle they had more information, though most of it was rumors.

''They say she fell in love with an Algerian boy in Paris,'' Baudou told me, ''when she was eighteen or nineteen. Henri found out. You can imagine how he took it, considering the National Front's anti-Arab policy. He tried to make Gabrielle drop the Algerian, but she wouldn't. Some people think he took the problem to his father. At any rate, it was thugs of the breed that gravitate to Jean-Louis's faction that jumped her boyfriend one night and beat him up. So badly that he later died in the hospital.''

Bertrand said, "Gabrielle didn't come back from Paris for almost half a year after that. She probably wouldn't have ever come back, except for her grandmother.

"There's one rumor," Bertrand added, "that Gabrielle stayed all that time in Paris because she had a nervous breakdown. Or something close to it. But if so, she had recovered by the time she returned. Fully, judging by how well she's doing at Taittinger.''

"Did they catch the ones who killed her boyfriend?'' I asked.

It was Baudou who answered. "Never. I guess Jean-Louis's contacts among the Paris police made sure of that.''

Before leaving Pommery I got the use of Bertrand's office phone for a call to Paris. They hadn't been able to give me anything about Angelina Doniol—and at that point she was one of my two possible leads to finding Sarah Byrne. The other was Henri. I was still concentrating on Henri, so for the moment I needed someone else checking further on Angelina.

Fritz Donhoff would have been perfect for that, but he was still comforting the Munich widow. I put the call through to Yann Cuchet, a former journalist turned investigator. We'd done business before, so I knew what I could trust him to handle properly. His specialty was divorce work, which made him perfect for this little job. I gave him Leon Doniol's Paris address and phone number, along with just enough information on Angelina Doniol to ensure that he'd ask the right questions.

"Try to get some answers tonight," I said, and I assured him my clients could manage his extra fee and expenses— if he didn't pad the latter with drinks for his friends at Maxim's.

Which reminded me I should phone my clients sometime tomorrow with whatever reassurance I could come up with by then to tide them over. So far all I had was that their daughter was alive and unharmed. Or had been when last I'd grabbed for her and missed.

Outside it had started raining again. Under the pall of low clouds, murky night was well advanced, although it was only a few minutes past seven. I did some careful checking before getting into my Renault. That story about Gabrielle's boyfriend being beaten to death had wiped out the relaxed feeling induced by the champagne. There were people in this town who didn't like me, and they could include some who'd been in on that nasty piece of work.

Nobody was watching the car and there was no indication anyone had messed with it. But after settling inside I considered whether it might not be a good idea to get the pistol I kept concealed in the car and stick it in my belt where I could get at it fast if I had to.

It was a short-barreled Mauser, strictly a close-quarters emergency weapon. The trouble was, if the emergency hit me abruptly and unexpectedly, it would take too long to get at it. I'd have to get down on one knee behind the front seat, reach under the back seat and up inside it to open the hidden compartment where the Mauser was tucked away. Awkward and time-consuming—but insurance against anyone else finding the gun short of doing a long, detailed strip-down search of the car.

A private detective in France doesn't have the right to carry a gun around with him. Keeping weapons at home is a different matter. A majority of the French have at least one "for the protection of domicile." But if you take it off your property it becomes illegal. The best you can get, if you apply to the authorities and can prove that your life is threatened in a specific situation, is a permit to carry a weapon for a strictly limited time period.

In my business, however, life-threatening situations crop up more often and more suddenly than for most normal citizens. And in France people believe in practicing what they call "System D." In essence, System D means doing whatever you can to detour around any uncomfortable government restrictions—and doing so in a way that cuts the hazard of getting caught at it as much as possible. Therefore I kept my gun in a place where it was difficult for me to get to it, but also difficult for a cop to find it.

If I transferred the Mauser from its hiding place to my person, the chance of getting caught with it increased sharply. It was one thing for somebody like Little Yuri to risk getting caught with a gun on him. The worst that France would do to a foreign agent, for that kind of infraction of the law, was to expel him from the country. After which he'd just get reassigned to a different country, or even return under another name. What they could do to me was to strip me of my right to carry on my business. Permanently.

I had to consider whether the present danger in Reims warranted that risk.

There was another consideration. French law says you can only use "equal force" to defend yourself. That applies to policemen as well as to private investigators and ordinary citizens. If a guy attacks you with a club you have no legal right to respond by shooting him, even if you think he intends to kill you with that club.

So far, the worst I'd been threatened with was brass knuckles. And the men who'd tried to take me in Les Tours had been amateurs. They might be tough, but they weren't qualified to handle anybody who'd ever gone through even a basic police course in street-survival skills. Let alone someone who'd had the kind of training you get before being turned loose as an undercover narc.

In the end I decided to leave the Mauser where it was when I headed off to pick up Gabrielle Lemaire. A few minutes later I was heartily grateful I'd chosen to do so.

I was driving into the center of Reims with my headlights pushing through the murk when it happened. Most of the downtown area had already closed down for the weekend and the streets had become empty and silent. I was some blocks from the Café du Palais when a police car cruised past me going in the opposite direction

It didn't go far. In my rearview mirror I saw it slow down behind me and then make a tight U-turn.

Then it came after me.

◙ 15 ◙

THE POLICE CAR didn't try to catch up with me. Not at first. It merely followed.

Keeping well below the city speed limit, I turned into the next cross street. It turned after me. I made another unnecessary turn. It was still there, half a block behind.

The next turn I took was in the direction of the Café du Palais. Slowing to a crawl when I reached it, I looked inside. There were a lot of people, but if Gabrielle was one of them I couldn't spot her. I cruised on, looking for a parking place. For two more blocks there was no legal spot in sight, and with the cop car on my tail I wasn't about to take any other kind.

Then I entered a big open square with a half-empty parking area on the other side of it. As I came to a halt there the police car rolled slowly past me.

It stopped in front of my car. Two uniformed members of the Municipal Police climbed out and strolled back to me as I got out of the Renault. One was carrying the stubby regulation submachine gun. The other said politely, "Turn and lean against your car, please."

I gave him my best innocent citizen smile. "What's the trouble, officer?"

"Routine check." They always say that, and usually it's the truth. All over the country they make hit-or-miss stops of nonlocal cars from time to time, hoping to come upon a wanted criminal or someone driving a stolen car. I was quite certain this wasn't one of those times.

I put my hands against the roof of the Renault and got frisked. "All right, your identity papers, please."

I gave him my passport, and my wallet opened to my international driver's license.

He looked at the passport first. "American?"

"Yes."

"But you are driving a car with Paris license plates. Rented?"

"No. It's registered and insured in my name." I gestured at the wallet. "You'll also find my French residence and work permits in there."

He didn't bother to look. "The papers of your car, please."

I reached in and got them out of the glove compartment. He gave them to the silent one with the submachine gun, who went back inside the police car with them. In routine checks they radio the information on your papers to their headquarters to make sure you and your car are clean. I still didn't think this was a routine check.

While the other cop waited with me he asked, "And what are you doing in Reims?"

"Seeing some people about business."

"What is your business?"

"It's all there in my wallet. I'm a licensed private investigator. I'm here searching for a runaway daughter."

"Ah? That's interesting."

It didn't sound as if he was at all interested. He was only making conversation while we waited, and after that he ran out of things to say. The waiting dragged on for about another five minutes before the other one returned from the police car. "All right," he told his partner.

My papers were returned to me. They both saluted me: polite gestures indicating I was cleared and dismissed. I watched with a crawly feeling as they got back into the police car and drove away. When their rear lights disappeared, I turned from the Renault and started walking in the opposite direction across the big square toward the café a few blocks back.

I was halfway across it when a Mercedes sedan shot out of a street to my left and sped straight across the square at me.

I shifted direction and ran. The Mercedes shifted, too, and came after me much faster than I could run. I heard its engine closing the gap behind me. There was no way I was going to get out of that square before that car hit me.

I changed direction again. Under the rubber soles of my shoes the uneven cobbles of the square were slick from the rain. I slipped, went down on one knee, and bounced back up, turning to face the oncoming Mercedes. Transfixed in its headlights, I threw up one arm to shield my eyes.

There were two figures in the front seat. I could only hope there weren't more in the back.

I waited as long as I dared before leaping aside. That let the driver see what had been hidden behind me: a hip-high steel post holding a public trash receptacle. It was too late by then for him to swerve around it. He jammed on the brakes, but the tires skidded on the wet cobbles. The Mercedes hurtled by me and crashed head-on into the post, bending it to the ground and coming to a jolting stop with the motor conking out.

The man beside the driver had been hurled forward, cracking the windshield with his head. The driver, though braced against the steering wheel, was shaken enough to be slow about throwing open his door. I was already there when he started to get out, leading the way with a fist holding a blackjack.

I rammed my heel against his door, putting all my weight behind the kick, before he could get any further out. He screamed as the bones in his forearm splintered. The scream went wild when I yanked him out of the car by that arm. He fell across the cobbles and I kicked him behind the ear before turning my back on him to look inside the Mercedes.

There was no one in the back seat. The man who'd cracked the windshield was slumped in the front moaning, blood trickling down his face. It was the younger of the two I'd tangled with in the brasserie. The one on the cobbles was the other. I saw something else, not unexpected: the Mercedes was equipped with a two-way radio.

I sprinted across the square to my Renault. The police car could be swinging back for a look by now. If I was lucky, Gabrielle Lemaire would be waiting for me inside the Café du Palais.

My luck was better than that. She was getting out of a taxi in front of the place when I drove up. She had changed into jeans, boots, and a scuffed leather jacket, and she was carrying a KLM flight bag. When I snapped at her to jump in she looked at my face and didn't ask why the hurry. She slid in beside me, calm but quick, shutting the door and tossing the bag in back while I gunned away.

She didn't say a word until we were out of the city and on the expressway to Paris. By then I'd stopped checking the rearview mirror so often.

"Feel better?" she asked me.

"A little. Not completely until we're in Paris. With that

comfortable feeling of having friends around to be called on when in need. Including some in the police.''

''What happened?''

So I told her. Piecing together the probable progression wasn't difficult: Jean-Louis phones Reims after I leave the Lemaire château and lets his people know he's worried I may still be hanging around, trying to dig up something about his son. After my tangle with the pair in Les Tours, they phone him. He gives instructions—to them and to two policemen he can trust. Having my car's description and license number makes it easy. The cop car and the Mercedes prowl around, looking for me and keeping in touch by radio. The cops find me and hold me in that square until the Mercedes is in position to do a job on me.

''Do you think they intended to kill you? Or just hurt you very badly?''

I glanced at her. ''Do you think they meant to kill your boyfriend?''

It broke her reserve for a moment. Then she got it back. At least in her expression. Her voice went a little ragged. ''So you found out about that.''

''My business is asking people about other people. You may have noticed.''

She was silent for a while. ''Youssef has been in his grave for almost six years now. So what difference does it make if that's what they were *supposed* to do to him?''

''You get the point. That's what can happen with thugs who aren't really professionals at just hurting. Sometimes they get excited and go too far. Afterward they're sorry. Killing a man is harder to cover up than only half killing him.''

Gabrielle was nodding. ''I'm certain Jean-Louis had a

difficult time making sure nothing happened to Henri after Youssef died.''

"Was Henri in on the beating?"

"I don't know, and that doesn't matter. I know he *caused* it. He warned me something like that would happen unless I stopped seeing Youssef. 'That dirty Arab,' he called him. I didn't stop. . . . So what happened is my fault, too.''

"Don't be stupid," I said, more sharply than I'd intended.

She looked at me, startled.

"Only stupid people do that," I told her. "They wonder what the victim of violence did to cause it instead of putting all the blame where it belongs: on the one who did it. Happens in everything from rape cases to genocide.''

"Except that *I* wasn't the victim. Youssef was.''

"So were you. It sounds to me like you still are, and six years is long enough to punish yourself for what you didn't do.''

Gabrielle fell silent, still looking at me.

I got off that uncomfortable subject and back to the one that concerned me. "You're right about one thing. It doesn't matter whether Henri actually took part in the beating. His father still had to cover up for the ones who did it. If they were caught and grilled hard enough, one of them might have broken down and told who they'd done it for. Jean-Louis had to make sure that didn't happen. Do you know who any of his police contacts in Paris are?''

"No. I only know that he does have some.''

"And he would have made sure they kept a protective eye on Henri after that," I thought out loud. "To warn his father if he was getting into more trouble.''

It had to be. It would explain why Henri was moving out, with Angelina Doniol and Sarah Byrne, the night I was on my way to his apartment. Commissaire Gojon's men knew I was hunting Sarah, who might be part of the Rue des Rosiers shooting. If none of them was in Jean-Louis's pocket, the word had spread to some cop who was. One who knew Sarah was involved with Henri Lemaire. He'd phoned a warning for Henri to get out of sight for awhile, either directly to Henri, or to Jean-Louis, who relayed the warning to his son.

Gabrielle got a snapshot out of her handbag. "Here's the picture of Henri you wanted."

"Thanks." I took it from her and slipped it into the inside pocket of my jacket with the photo of Angelina Doniol: the teacher on whom he'd had a teenage crush and with whom he was now deeply involved on at least one level.

It was about five minutes since I'd last had a look at the rearview mirror. I checked again and relaxed another notch. We were halfway to Paris. None of Jean-Louis's local muscle was going to chase after me beyond that. It was too far out of the area where their own people could give them protection.

"Tell me something," I asked her. "Why do you stick around your family, feeling the way you do?"

"My grandmother needs somebody who cares checking from time to time to make sure she's all right."

"Have you thought about what you'll do after she dies?"

"Of course. I'll move away. I have a regular and substantial income from the family business. There's nothing my uncle and cousin can do to stop that."

"Where will you go? Paris?"

"No, to some area where I can reinvolve myself in what I know best: the wine business."

"You ought to look around in the south, where I live.

The wine business there is starting to expand. I've thought about getting into it myself.''

"Between driving in rallies and prying into the more painful parts of people's lives?''

"It *would* make for busy days," I acknowledged.

"There *are* some good wines from the south," she said diplomatically. "Depends how far south you mean. Where do you live?''

I told her about the house.

"I know the area fairly well," Gabrielle said. "The usual holidays. St. Tropez, Cannes, Monaco. I like it, except in July and August, when half of France pours down there to the beaches.''

"That's when you go up in the mountains just behind the coast. The tourists miss that part, and it's beautiful. With lots of uncultivated land just waiting to be turned into vineyards.''

"They don't produce good wine that close to the coast.''

"There you're wrong. What you mean is they don't dump in enough chemical additives to preserve their wine for long voyages. And one reason they don't is because most of it's already selling so well locally.''

"It's always interesting to be shown something new," she said. "Perhaps I'll come visit you sometime.''

I shot her a quick glance. But all I saw in her expression was that ladylike poise.

She switched on my car radio and turned it to France Musique. "Do you mind?''

"No." The station was into the final scenes of *Turandot*, and I'd gotten addicted to Puccini early on. My American grandmother was an opera fan and my grandfather had learned to enjoy listening to her records when he'd had a few drinks and before he'd had too many.

Gabrielle Lemaire rested her head against the top of the seat and soaked up Puccini for a while. Then she said, "Your house down there must be quite close to where Grace Kelly got killed driving off that mountain road."

I nodded. "About two kilometers directly below it. I guess a lot of people have said you look like her."

"Yes. Is it true what some people say—that she'd had too much to drink and that's why it happened?"

"No."

"Then why do people say it?"

"Because they relish nastiness about anybody who's well-known. They've got low opinions of themselves and don't know what to do about it except to try dragging everybody else's reputation down to their level."

"You have a rather disenchanted view of humanity."

"Cops and lawyers tend to get that way. They see too much." We were entering the outskirts of Paris. "Where does your father live?"

"Rue Rembrandt, on the south side of parc Monceau. My apartment is there, too. Actually, it's a few rooms I've taken over on the top floor of his townhouse, overlooking the park."

"At least I won't have to change into my slumming costume."

She laughed. "It *is* a good address," she admitted.

Indeed. Fashionable Parisian society is strict about what can be considered a desirable address. The ile St. Louis is good. Avenue Foch is better. The quarter immediately around Parc Monceau is one of the very best. The Soviet Union, ever sensitive to such nuances, established its Paris consulate as close as it could to Parc Monceau.

I drove in that direction as *Turandot* ended and France Musique started its news summary.

In Beirut the Moslems had taken a break from killing Christians and were back to killing one another.

In Brussels the French delegation to the European Economic Community was insisting on higher subsidies for the farmers of France.

In Paris the police had arrested a young man who was believed to have taken part in the terrorist shooting in the Rue des Rosiers.

The accused terrorist had not been identified as yet. At least not to the news media.

"I STOLE IT," Benito Santato repeated for the third time since I'd gotten there.

He'd been saying the same to Commissaire Gojon for some two hours before I'd arrived. He wasn't forthcoming with much of anything else, including how long he'd been in France or who his contacts were in Paris. A cool customer with nothing to indicate that any kind of approach was likely to crack his hard shell.

Benito Santato was a member of the Brigades Rouge, wanted by the Italian police in connection with some political kidnappings and several murders in Milan. He was about twenty-eight, short and stocky, with close-cropped reddish hair and pale gray eyes that stared back at Gojon without blinking. When he spoke it was in a university-educated French with only a trace of an Italian accent. He didn't speak often.

Gojon had both hands pressed flat on his desk in an effort to control his temper. Santato sat on a metal stool on the other side of the desk, his left wrist handcuffed to the cast-iron radiator against the wall behind him. I stood against the closed door of Gojon's office and watched while he tried variations on his list of questions and threats. Santato took both with an expression as giving as a clenched fist.

He had been using false identity papers in France. He'd been picked up by a pair of detectives who'd been sent to watch his apartment building and question him when he showed up there. Originally just because he was rumored to have been seen occasionally with Fernand Claudel, the terrorist Little Yuri had killed at the Rue des Rosiers. They'd felt justified in taking him into custody and having a look inside his apartment because he'd arrived driving a motorcycle with the license number I'd given to Gojon.

Henri Lemaire's motorcycle.

At first Santato had claimed to have borrowed it from an unnamed friend. But after they'd found what was in his apartment he'd switched to saying he'd stolen the motorcycle off the street. He claimed never to have heard of Henri Lemaire.

"And the trunkload of weapons we found in your place," Gojon said thinly. "Two AK-47 automatic assault rifles, one of them from Bulgaria and the other the Finnish Valmet variation. A pump-action shotgun. Three revolvers and two pistols. Ammunition for all of it. Did you steal those also? Or merely borrow them?"

"I didn't know what was in the trunk," Santato answered, sounding bored. "Somebody asked me to keep it for him for a while. I never looked inside it."

"Who is this somebody?"

Santato shrugged. "A man I met in a bar. Never met him before; haven't seen him since."

"Describe him."

"Skinny guy with glasses, brown hair starting to go bald."

Gojon's face darkened. Santato was describing *him*. He took a moment to keep his voice quiet and steady. "Where were you yesterday between noon and two in the afternoon?"

"Taking a walk."

"Where? Who saw you?"

Another shrug. "Along the river. Right Bank. I don't know who saw me. I didn't see anybody I knew. But that's where I was. You can't prove I had anything to do with what happened at the Rue des Rosiers."

Commissaire Gojon's hands clenched on his desk. I watched him force them open, make the fingers relax. When he spoke again his voice was even quieter. "The Italian police want you. If we turn you over to them you'll spend the rest of your life in prison for murder and kidnapping. On the other hand, we can keep you here in France on our own charges, refuse to allow extradition to Italy. At the moment you're only charged with using false papers and illegal possession of forbidden types of arms. Cooperate with me and we won't try too hard to prove you took part in the attack yesterday. The worst you'll get is a few years."

Santato looked bored and said nothing.

Gojon's voice became so quiet it was barely above a whisper. "Don't cooperate and we'll ship you back to Italy a cripple."

Santato continued to look bored. Gojon waited and he waited and I waited. The clock between the two telephones on Gojon's desk ticked loudly.

The door behind me opened, bumping against my back. I stepped aside and a commissaire from another branch of the French police system barged in: Jules Emeric of the Brigade Criminelle.

He was a heavyset man with a beefy face and mean eyes. We had met briefly several times in the past. I had no specific reason to dislike him. On the other hand, I had no reason to like him, either. On appearance and manner alone I preferred not to until proved wrong.

Emeric started to brandish an official document of some

sort at Gojon. Then he stopped and scowled at me. The scowl switched back to Gojon. "What is *he* doing here?"

Gojon nodded at me. "Wait outside in the corridor."

Stepping out, I shut his office door behind me and leaned against the corridor wall. I could make an educated guess about what was going on based on the fact that Gojon's Brigade d'Intervention and Emeric's Brigade Criminelle were unfriendly rivals and both were supposed to deal with terrorism.

In fact, all of the many branches of the French police system hate one another and frequently and deliberately step on one another's toes. They've been known to let a wanted criminal escape rather than allow him to be taken by a rival department. The car radios of different branches can't even communicate with one another.

The original theory behind this uncooperative diversity was that it would prevent the police from ever getting together to overthrow the government. An interesting idea that made for lousy police work.

My hunch was that Emeric and Gojon were fighting over custody of Benito Santato. Judging by the way Emeric had brandished that official document, he was probably emerging the victor. Which wouldn't be good for me. I'd established a relationship of guarded mutual trust with Gojon. And nothing with Emeric.

There wasn't anything I could do about it except wait to find out.

I wondered if Gabrielle Lemaire was finding out anything of use to me.

I had dropped her off at the elegant townhouse on Parc Monceau minutes after hearing the news broadcast about the capture of the unnamed terrorist. My discussion with her father, I'd decided, could wait until later that night or the next day. Finding out what Gojon had learned was more urgent.

We'd exchanged telephone numbers and Gabrielle had promised to explain about me to her father before she went off to a party she'd been invited to that night. "You could join me there later," she'd suggested, "if you get free in time."

She was full of surprises. "Thanks for the invitation, but I doubt if I'll be able to."

"You won't be missing much if you don't come. Except a chance to keep me from being bored to death. A lot of very dull young idle rich will be there. I've been going to stupid parties like this almost every weekend for the last year. It's my analyst's idea. A way of opening myself up to life again. In a way she's right. Most of the types I meet at these things make me feel like a dynamo in comparison."

Then she'd cocked her head at me and added, "Some of the ones tonight have known Henri a long time. I could find out if any of them have been seeing him recently."

"I'd appreciate any help you can give me."

"If I go on being your assistant like this you'll have to start paying me."

"You're already getting what you want out of it."

"A chance at revenge for what happened to Youssef, you mean?"

"More than that. You're hoping I'll prove something against your cousin Henri that puts him in prison for a long time. That way he won't wind up running the family firm. You will."

"There's that possibility," she'd acknowledged evenly.

She'd given me a phone number where I could reach her

at the party that night, just in case, before I'd driven off to see Commissaire Gojon.

I stood in the corridor outside Gojon's office while the waiting dragged on and his door remained shut. Emeric had been closeted in there with him and Benito Santato for over fifteen minutes now. Gojon was probably on the phone to his superiors, as high up as he could get, trying to keep Emeric from snatching Santato away from him. Whether he won or lost, it was going to take time. It was getting late, I was hungry, and I had at least one urgent phone call to make.

I walked off along the corridor between the glass-fronted offices of Gojon's adjutant commissaire and chief inspector, past the big room where his inspectors had their desks, down the stairs, and out of the building. There was a good brasserie called the Sports Bar half a block away. I had a hardboiled egg and glass of red at the bar while the bartender fixed me a sandwich of Périgord pâté on crusty brown bread.

The phone booth was in the back. I sat down inside it with my sandwich, took a bite, and then dialed the direct line into Gojon's office. The pâté was delicious. Gojon's line was busy.

I ate another bite of my sandwich and dialed Yann Cuchet's home number to find out what he had for me on Angelina Doniol.

⊠ **17** ⊠

"I'M IN THE middle of a late dinner," Yann told me.

"So am I. What did you get?"

Behind him his wife was yelling, "Tell him you'll call him back after we finish eating!"

I threatened him: "You want me to take my time about getting your fee to you?"

Yann shouted at his wife, "Shut up and put it back in the oven!" To me he said, "I spent almost an hour with Leon Doniol right after you called me. He was on his way to a local bar for a drink when I got there, so I went with him and bought him a few to loosen him up. That'll be on my bill. His drinks and mine."

"Naturally."

"Plus I got a parking ticket on my car while I was in the bar with him. That'll be on my bill, too."

I took another bite of my sandwich and waited for him to get on with it.

"Okay," Yann said briskly. "This Leon Doniol is a sweet guy, but soft. I gave him the stuff about looking for his wife, Angelina, because of an inheritance, but it didn't matter if he believed it. He was just happy to talk to somebody about her. Even after all this time. He said when I find her to tell her he's still ready to take her back. She must be something special. Leon doesn't strike me as a guy who can't find another girl to move in with him."

"He doesn't know where she is."

"No, but he thinks she went off to Germany with another guy she met. The thing is, after Leon and Angelina moved to Paris, she got a job teaching German and French at Berlitz. One of her students was this guy named Martin Droscher, from Germany. He enrolled at Berlitz to learn French. Droscher and Angelina fell for each other and off they went."

"Where does this Martin Droscher live?"

"Doniol doesn't know. So I went to Berlitz. They're open late for people who can only go at night. Lots of people—"

"Just tell me what you found out, Yann."

"I had to bribe a secretary in the office to get a look at their books. A hundred francs. And I got another parking ticket outside Berlitz."

"That had better be all. You're not allowed more than two tickets in one night on a job this small."

"Two is all I got. Okay, get a pencil." When I had my notebook and ballpoint ready he told me the home address in Stuttgart that Martin Droscher had given when he'd registered for the Berlitz course. Yann also had his birth date: it would make Droscher thirty-nine.

"Where was he living in Paris?" I asked.

"A sublet near Place d'Italie, but I already checked there. Droscher moved out shortly after Angelina Doniol quit her job at Berlitz. I talked to a couple that live across the landing from the apartment he sublet. They say he went home to Stuttgart. There was a woman who lived with him the last couple weeks before he left who fits the description of Angelina. They think she went with him. To Germany. That's it. I think I did a good, fast job for you, true?"

"You got a fast couple parking tickets while you were at it."

"I'll mail you my bill first thing in the morning."

We both hung up. I finished my sandwich and dialed Gojon's office. Still busy, or busy again. The Sports Bar cashier arranged for me to put through a long-distance call to Munich. I made it person to person. The widow Fritz Donhoff was staying with didn't speak any French at all, and my German is rudimentary.

"I hope you're ready to go back to work," I told Fritz when I got him on the line. "Starting tomorrow."

"All good things must end," Fritz said in that rumbling bass of his. "If you really need me I can't say no."

It sounded to me as if he'd had enough of the soft life with the pretty widow and had been waiting for a decent excuse to cut out. Old Fritz was like that. He'd never been married. He explained it as being realistic about himself. Flirtation was in his blood. He enjoyed women and they enjoyed him. He was seventy-three and the combination of his voice, genuine human warmth, and old world charm could still turn women between twenty and eighty to jelly.

I gave him a fast rundown on the situation and told him all about Angelina Reisler Doniol and what little I had on Martin Droscher.

Fritz repeated the name slowly: "Martin Droscher . . . that has a familiar ring, somehow. I'll have to think about it, give it a little time. My memory is not what it once was, you know."

"Yeah, I know. You're into an advanced stage of senility." Fritz's memory was better than mine. Also he knew more than I did and had more useful contacts. What I'd brought to the partnership was an ability to move around easier and faster than he could.

"How are your police connections in Stuttgart these days?" I asked him.

"Excellent. And, of course, Stuttgart is quite close to Munich. I'll drive there in the morning."

"First go out to the airport. Check on the earliest flight from Paris into Munich. I'll arrange for a stewardess to bring a picture of Angelina Doniol."

"Tell her I'll be wearing a red carnation on my lapel."

"I'll tell her you'll be the most distinguished-looking dirty old man in sight. Kiss the widow good-bye for me."

"Indeed I will, Peter. And how is *your* romance progressing?"

"She got transferred to Bolivia."

"Temporarily?"

"I hope so."

"Don't sit around and brood about it, Pierre-Ange. Get back in the swim immediately. I don't like that 'poor me' sound in your voice."

"Go to hell," I told him.

"Now you sound better," Fritz said. "Wherever I do go, I'll let you know as soon as I turn up anything."

After breaking the connection I tried Gojon's office again. Busy. I dialed the number Gabrielle Lemaire had given me for the party. A girl finally answered the phone there. She had to speak very loudly for me to hear her. Somewhere not far from her an old Pink Floyd record was being played at top volume. She said she'd find Gabrielle for me. I listened to Pink Floyd and some drunken shouting while I waited. The party might be boring, but it wasn't quiet.

Gabrielle came on the line. "Hold on while I carry this into the bedroom. It's got a long extension cord." There was the sound of a door being slammed shut and the noise of the party became a dim background. "That's better. Are you coming?"

"Can't make it."

"Oh. I was depending on you to save me."

"Bad as that?"

"I've got to talk to my analyst about whether anything this bad can really be good for me. If you're calling about my father, he wasn't home. Left word he'll be back sometime tomorrow."

"Anybody at that party have anything recent and pertinent on Henri?"

"I've just started trying to find out. I'm new at this detective business, remember. Give me time; I'll learn."

"I'll phone you tomorrow."

"I've got my weekly session with my analyst tomorrow morning. And a date from late afternoon into the evening. Between the two we could have lunch. By then my father should be home or I'll know when he will be."

We agreed to decide where and when to lunch when we got in touch by phone the next day. I hung up and tried Gojon's office. This time I got him.

"What's happening?" I asked him.

"Where are you?" He sounded tired.

"Sports Bar."

"Order me spaghetti bolognese and a demi. I'll be there in a few minutes."

I was waiting in a corner booth when Gojon came in. Our meals were brought to the table as he settled down across from me. I'd ordered myself a steak and salad. The sandwich had been delicious but not enough. We concentrated on eating for a while before talking shop.

"Good meat," I said finally. "Tender."

"Everything is good here, but I'm getting tired of it. I've eaten here almost every night for the last two weeks."

"Doesn't your wife feed you anymore?"

"She doesn't do anything for me anymore. She's left me."

I thought about Maidi and commiserated with a fellow sufferer. "Sorry to hear it. I know how you feel."

"Do you? Oh, yes, I remember now—perhaps you do." He didn't know about Maidi, so he had to be referring to some years back. Sure enough: "I heard you were once married and it broke up. I never learned why."

I shrugged. "We had a good year and then a couple of bad ones. In the beginning she found the French side of my nature fascinating. In the end she found my attitudes *too* French. Said it confused her."

"Ah, you married an American. Perhaps that was your mistake. I've wondered, do *you* feel French, or American?"

"Depends where I am. In America I feel French. Here I feel American."

"That must make your emotional life complicated. Or does it make life more interesting?"

"A little of both."

"And French women—do they find you fascinating because you're American? And then discover you are *too* American?"

"When people become uncomfortable with each other," I said, "they can always come up with reasons for it. Not always the real reasons."

Gojon nodded sagely. "My wife has left me for a devout Catholic who has a wife and four children. She says she needs the experience of being someone's mistress. She feels she married too young and missed all the delights and pangs of amorous adventures."

He grimaced, looking more annoyed than bereft by it. I

gave him time to get more off his chest if he wanted to, but he devoted himself to his eating.

I finished off my steak and sipped my wine. "You lost Santato?"

"Yes, but not to Emeric, at least. My director general worked out a compromise with the head of Emeric's brigade and the chief of the Alphabet Soup."

Alphabet Soup is one of the easier ways of referring to a branch of the police with a name so long even its members have difficulty remembering all of it. Even its initials: O.C.R.T.I.A.M.E.M.S. They stand for Central Office for the Repression of Illicit Traffic in Arms, Munitions, Explosives, and other Sensitive Materials. What that involved name adds up to is yet another department supposed to operate against terrorists.

"Benito Santato has been turned over to the Alphabet Soup," I hazarded.

Gojon nodded, finished eating, and called for another beer. "They won't get anything out of him."

"You wouldn't have, either. Even if you'd bounced him off the walls for the next week."

"Probably not, but I'd have enjoyed the attempt." Gojon eyed me narrowly, back in business, companionable chatter about runaway wives forgotten. "You knew that motorcycle belonged to Henri Lemaire when you gave me its license number."

I dodged that with a question. "What does Henri Lemaire have to say about a Brigades Rouge terrorist using his motorcycle? Lent or stolen?"

"We haven't been able to locate him yet to ask. He doesn't seem to be using his apartment at the moment."

"You could try his family home outside Reims."

"I did. A few hours ago. *After* Santato was captured in

possession of Henri Lemaire's motorcycle. Until then I had only your unsubstantiated suggestion that that particular motorcycle *might* have been used by the terrorists involved in the Rue des Rosiers attack.''

Gojon was speaking slowly and quietly, testing each word. Police officers don't advance in their careers unless they show an appreciation of the need to tread softly wherever prominent people are involved.

I said, ''You proceeded with due care.''

''*Great* care,'' Gojon agreed evenly. ''Especially with Emeric and his boys keeping tabs on every move I make. Along with the people from the Alphabet Soup. Both of which groups showed up to take over at the Rue des Rosiers shortly after you left there.''

''And since then it's become a three-cornered tug-of-war over which of you is in charge of the case.''

''At this point all three of us seem to be.'' Gojon made sure his voice didn't carry beyond our booth. ''And Commissaire Emeric happens to be politically friendly with Jean-Louis Lemaire.''

''Ah,'' I said. I felt like saying it again but restrained myself. ''How long did it take Emeric to find out I'd been at the Rue des Rosiers looking for Sarah Byrne?''

''Not long, I should imagine. His boys questioned everybody who was still there. Also, I'm almost certain he has a spy planted among my men.''

''Does Emeric know Henri Lemaire, as well as his father?''

''I have reason to believe he does.''

One of the questions that had been nagging at me was answered. I was sure of it: Emeric was the reason Henri had been vacating his apartment, along with Sarah and Angelina Doniol, by the time I'd gotten there.

"So you finally felt you had enough justification to make one careful phone call to Reims," I prodded. "Spoke to the head of the family himself, I imagine?" Gojon nodded. "Who told you what?"

"Jean-Louis Lemaire has no idea exactly where his son might be at the moment," Gojon said, poker-faced. "He doesn't keep a close watch over the boy. Believes in letting a young man feel a sense of independence. He did remember that the last time he spoke to his son, the young man mentioned something about his motorcycle being missing. And that he intended to report it to the police. But he has apparently not gotten around to doing so, so far. Other things on his mind, you understand. Love affairs and other sundry youthful follies."

We smiled at each other understandingly.

I asked him, "Have you had a look inside Henri Lemaire's apartment?"

"Oddly enough," Gojon told me blandly, "two of my men had occasion to, this afternoon. There was a call from one of his neighbors, who refused to identify herself, that she heard someone attempting to break into his place."

It was one way to sidestep having to officially apply for a warrant to force entry into the residence of an important man's son.

"My men found that his apartment door *had* been broken open."

"So they went inside to capture the culprit."

"Precisely. Unfortunately, the robber had already fled. He must have heard them enter the building. Fortunately, it seems he didn't have enough time to steal anything. There doesn't seem to be anything missing. So our prompt response to the call did serve a purpose."

It would stand up, put that way, if he were questioned about his reasons for entering the apartment.

"Anything interesting among the stuff that wasn't missing?"

Gojon permitted himself a small smile. "You mean such as his address book?"

"Or some such."

"Nothing of interest." Gojon drank half of his second beer and placed the glass back on the table between us delicately. "All right, Sawyer. Your turn to tell me what's going on. Have your Arab friends come up with any other friends of the late Fernand Claudel? His Libyan contacts? Or his movements over the week or so before Yuri Suchar shot him?"

"Nothing so far. I'll check again in the morning and let you know if I get anything at all. Speaking of Little Yuri, do you know where I can find him these days? He shifts living quarters pretty often, and I've been away from Paris for months."

"You would have to go some distance to find him at the moment," Gojon told me. "Commissaire Emeric found some witnesses who told him about a man of Yuri's description whom they saw run across the Rue des Rosiers carrying a handgun. Naturally Emeric went to call on him, since his carrying of such a weapon would be illegal."

Gojon had gone poker-faced again. "However, someone seems to have alerted Yuri Suchar. By the time Emeric located his current residence, Yuri Suchar was taking a plane back to Israel. I doubt that he'll return for some time."

I said it again: "Ah."

"Yes." Gojon picked up his glass and began tapping it lightly on the table while he eyed me with something approaching the way he'd looked at Benito Santato. "And have you found out anything more about this American girl you were searching for?"

I had to give him *something*. "I found her," I said. "And lost her." I told him all about my encounter with Sarah Byrne. And Henri Lemaire. *And* the tall woman Little Yuri and I had seen behind the Rue des Rosiers.

Gojon's eyes, slightly magnified behind his glasses, fastened on me like those of a surgeon preparing to make a deep incision. "I warned you to notify me *immediately* if you turned up anything." His face was dark with anger.

"I gave you that motorcycle number," I reminded him. "Without that your men would never have arrested Santato and searched his place and found those guns. They'd just have questioned him about Fernand Claudel and let him go."

"Is that supposed to compensate for what you held out on me? It *does not*."

"I've also just told you that Henri Lemaire is almost certainly one of the terrorist gang you're looking for. Are you going to launch an official manhunt for him now?"

Gojon's eyes suddenly began avoiding mine. He still wasn't prepared to go up against a man as powerful as Jean-Louis Lemaire by doing something like that. It's a curious fact of life: men with the guts to risk their lives to do their duty will shrink from doing what they know they should if it jeopardizes their jobs or careers.

"You mean because he was with that woman," he said evasively. His tone had lost its cutting edge.

"That's what I mean." We both knew he wasn't going to go after Jean-Louis Lemaire's son. Not at this point.

And because shrinking from it embarrassed him, he was going to let me off the hook. For the moment.

"She does sound like the woman Yuri said took part in the attack," Gojon acknowledged cautiously.

"Took part in it, hell," I told him flatly. "I think she was the one who *led* it."

I didn't tell him her name or show him her picture. I wanted Fritz Donhoff to stay a few steps ahead of the police in helping me locate Angelina Doniol. Because she was turning into my best lead so far.

I needed to get hold of Sarah Byrne before anyone else—with enough of a time-edge to determine for myself her degree of innocence or guilt.

There was no way I could know at that point that the reason for what I was doing was already in the process of shifting drastically on me.

▩ **18** ▩

"THE MOST RECENT item I was able to dig up on Henri is a couple weeks old," Gabrielle told me. "But it may be pertinent. From Adrianne de Montelor. She's from Reims, went to school with Henri and me. Moved to Paris when she married a middle-aged duke who's one of the Finance Ministry's decision makers. Probably why our economy's in its current shape. After they divorced, Adrianne stayed on here. If you saw the Ile St. Louis apartment he had to turn over to her as part of their divorce settlement, you'd understand why."

"That's where your party was last night?"

"You're a good guesser." She gave me one of those appraising looks I was getting used to. "Among your other qualities." She hesitated and then asked, "Have you ever killed anybody?"

"Yes."

She sat up a little straighter and her moody brown eyes got a little brighter. "Tell me about it."

"No," I said flatly. And then: "Tell me about Henri."

We were lunching at one of the terrace tables of a seafood restaurant on the Quai Voltaire, with a view across the river of the Louvre and the Jardin du Carrousel. She had chosen the place for our lunch because she'd arranged for her date to pick her up there. It was a good Saturday for outdoor dining. The Paris air was warm but not too hot, and the pink-and-blue striped awning shielded our eyes from the strong sunlight. Gabrielle had ordered a big bowl of moules marinières and was polishing them off with a healthy appetite. I was having a mixed platter of oysters, shrimps, and crab. Flowers bloomed in green pots beside our table. Barges pushed past on the Seine, going to and from the Paris end of the canal system that still carries much of the cargo traffic throughout Europe.

Peaceful.

It had been a busy Saturday morning for me. Up early to get copies made of the photographs of Henri Lemaire and Angelina Doniol. Out to the airport in time to pay a Lufthansa stewardess to deliver one of Angelina Doniol to Fritz on the first flight to Munich. Then back into the Barbes-Rochechouart district for another talk with Mussa ben Zaer.

Mussa hadn't had any luck so far in finding anyone who recognized the photos of Fernand Claudel and Sarah Byrne. I could only hope he'd get luckier with the two new pictures I left with him: Henri Lemaire and Angelina Doniol.

Back to my apartment for that long-distance call I didn't really want to make to Sarah Byrne's parents. This time it had been Maureen Byrne who'd gotten on the phone with me. She hadn't been cheered by the news that I'd seen and talked to her daughter briefly before the girl had slipped away from me.

I didn't explain how she had slipped away. "I couldn't hold on to her by force. No justification for it. Your daughter looks well and reasonably contented. She said to tell you she needs time to make her own life."

"*Is* she in trouble?"

I couldn't say that she wasn't. The best I could tell Maureen Byrne was that Sarah hadn't acted as if she *thought* she was in trouble.

"Please try to find her again, Mr. Sawyer. And *try* to persuade her to meet with us when we get to Paris. We've given Rochefort instructions to pay you whatever you need, whenever you wish."

I'd hung up with the hope but no assurance that I was going to earn my money.

When I'd picked Gabrielle up at the Parc Monceau townhouse she told me that her father and one of his two current mistresses hadn't gotten home until after six that morning and were both still sleeping it off.

"They were at some all-night *partouze*." A *partouze* is usually some jet-set variation on an orgy, generally with gimmicks thrown in to give jaded French high-society types some zest in their lives. "I think this was one of the kind where all the men drop their visiting cards in a hat and their mistresses or wives go with the man whose card they pull out."

"And if they get the card of their own man they just toss it back in and try again."

Gabrielle nodded. "A bit sad, isn't it?"

"I imagine that depends on who you wind up with. It beats driving your car into a tree for kicks."

"You think I should try *partouze* hopping instead?"

"I think you're old enough to make those decisions for yourself. When do you think your father will be in shape to see me?"

"I left a note that you'll be there to talk to him this afternoon between two and three. He *should* be all right by then. . . ." Her frown was worried. "The problem is that he's begun drinking too much when he goes to a *partouze*. *And* snorting cocaine. Because he's afraid he's becoming impotent."

"Your father's pretty frank with you."

"Not about things like that. I get it from his girlfriends. He's always horribly embarrassed when I find out what he's doing. I've tried to explain to him that he shouldn't be. I'm not a child. And going to that kind of party isn't anything he has to be guilty about in front of me. He's not *hurting* anybody. Except perhaps himself, in the long run."

Her date was supposed to pick her up at the restaurant on the quay at two. We still had almost an hour to go when she spilled what she'd heard about her cousin Henri the night before.

"Adrianne saw him some weeks ago. He was having lunch with a woman outside a brasserie on Avenue Secretan. Adrianne was surprised when she recognized the woman he was with. Guess who."

"Angelina Doniol?"

"Right again."

Avenue Secretan is a wide tree-lined street of middle- and lower-class shops, bars, and restaurants that angles from the barge canals to Parc des Buttes Chaumont, way up in a northeast section of the city. It's a busy street, always crowded with local people. You don't see tourists there, and you don't expect to meet an ex-duchess, either.

"What was your friend doing there?"

"Adrianne's maid was going through an illness, and that's where she lives. A Portuguese woman. Adrianne went to see her, bring her some medicine, and make sure she didn't need anything else. Adrianne is not the brightest person, but she is kind and generous. She'd left her maid's place and was looking for a taxi when she spotted Henri with Angelina."

"Did she talk to them?"

"Oh, sure—Adrianne has too much curiosity not to. She says Angelina seemed to be laying down the law to Henri as she approached their table. Rather sternly, the way she used to when we were students and she was our teacher. And Henri was taking it like a lamb, looking at her as though she were some kind of goddess. Angelina always had that ability to dominate people.

"Angelina didn't recognize Adrianne at first. But Henri reminded her Adrianne used to be in one of her classes in Reims. Angelina remembered her then, but she didn't ask her to join them. Henri started to and then shut up. Adrianne had a feeling Angelina kicked him under the table.

"She told them she was surprised they'd gone on seeing each other all these years. Henri said they hadn't. That they hadn't seen each other in years until they ran into each other by chance in Paris about four months ago, after Angelina had returned to France following some time in Germany. And—they'd renewed old acquaintances."

"That's what Henri had to say. What did Angelina Doniol say?"

"Not much. She just sat there, obviously waiting for Adrianne to go away. Which she did, after she became embarrassed about standing at their table and not being asked to sit down."

"That's all of it?"

Gabrielle nodded. "Except that Adrianne got a very strong feeling that Henri's still crazy about Angelina. Or crazy about her again. Of course, everybody at school knew he had that crush on her. But he was a kid then. Now he's in his twenties—and Angelina must be more than ten years older than he is. But according to Adrianne, she's as striking-looking and sure of herself as ever. . . . Does any of this help you at all?"

"It clears up some dim corners a little. What's the name of the brasserie where your friend saw them?"

"I asked her that, but she didn't notice it. She says it's on the corner at the very end of Avenue Secretan by the Juan Juarès Métro station."

That put it on the east edge of Mussa ben Zaer's neighborhood.

Gabrielle asked archly, "Well, did I at least earn my lunch?"

"You did fine. You can even have some dessert."

She had a rich, throaty laugh. I hadn't heard it before. It did things to me. I'd already decided to be wary of that.

"My analyst approves of you," she said suddenly, startling me.

"Your analyst doesn't know me."

"She knows what I told her this morning."

"You don't know me, either."

"That can be remedied. Joel is taking me to his place outside Paris. He has his own stables there. Other people are joining us. We'll ride his horses and then have dinner. . . . I *could* get back in time to see you again tonight."

In France there was probably never a time when eyebrows would have been raised by a woman initiating a relationship with a man. In the States younger women have become much freer about that than their mothers and grandmothers were. But it *is* a break with old conventions, and they tend to be aware of that. Whereas for Frenchwomen it is a continuation of certain basic traditions that give them greater self-confidence on a variety of levels. It comes of the French, male and female, growing up in a society where the ability of women to deal with practical matters better than men is a given fact of taught history.

Other countries would consider Napoleon their greatest general. In France he's only second-best. The most important military leader of French history, of course, is a young girl named Jeanne d'Arc. She certainly had a more permanent effect on the nation's destiny.

Every schoolchild learns that the mistresses of the kings of France were not Barbie dolls, like those of the kings in England. Often they were not even pretty, and it was not unusual for them to be older than the kings they served. What they did have was extraordinary charm and the strength of character and intelligence to become the most valued political advisers of their kings.

You see the results today in any mom-and-pop store in France. Go into a bakery, and it's the wife you'll find handling the customers and the cash register; her husband's hidden away, doing the baking.

"I don't know what tonight has in store for me yet," I told her. "You can phone me. If I'm not there, leave a message on the machine."

She smiled and asked me, "Is that a rejection?"

Only women who look that good can put that question with a smile.

I said, "Has any man ever rejected you?"

"It would be a novel experience," she admitted. "Perhaps good for me. But I'd prefer not having it with you."

It was flattering and undeniably exciting. I couldn't help wanting her. It would ease the sense of loss and loneliness I was still trying to deal with, at least temporarily. But Gabrielle Lemaire was very young; and under that self-assurance, she was fragile.

And for me, it was too soon after Maidi. You meet someone and become lovers, and if it works you become a pair. A team; a couple. If it breaks, you need time to get over needing that particular person. You look for what she was in anybody new. And it's not there.

On the other hand . . .

"Why does your analyst approve of me?"

"From what I told her, she thinks you might be good therapy for me. So do I."

"I'm not a medical prescription, Gabrielle. I'm just a man. With a man's normal hungers."

"I noticed that the first time you looked at me. I'll call you tonight. I hope you'll be there."

We were finishing our coffees and desserts (*crème caramel* for her, *poire Belle Hélène* for me) when a brand-new red Lancia sports car pulled over to the curb in front of us. The casually dressed man who climbed out was in his mid-twenties, tall and wiry. He strode over to our table. A handsome devil with a fierce beak of a nose. He gave me a noncommittal nod and bent toward Gabrielle, letting her decide how much kiss to put into their greeting.

Public kissing in France has precise nuances. One kiss on the cheek is just ordinary politeness between people who know each other. Greeting someone with kisses on both cheeks denotes genuine fondness. Usually it's just cheek to cheek. A real kiss, applying lips to cheek, indicates a greater degree of affection. It can go up to four kisses, on alternate cheeks. A kiss on the mouth is a statement of passion.

Gabrielle applied her cheek to his left cheekbone and then gave his right cheek a tentative peck with her lips. Anyone could read that: she felt something for him, but was still unsure what.

She said, "You're a bit early, Joel."

He took the hint, gave me another nod, and went back to the Lancia. After getting in he sat waiting with his hands on the wheel, looking straight ahead, not at us. Good manners.

Gabrielle rested a hand on mine. "Don't worry," she said, as though she'd been reading my mind earlier. "I won't break as easily as you think. I'm not *that* delicate."

My supply of stoic resolve has its limits. I said, "Call me."

"I will." She took her shoulder bag and stood up, leaned down, and kissed me on both cheeks. With her lips.

She crossed the sidewalk and got into the red Lancia. Joel drove her away, turning to cross the Pont Royal. The car was lost to sight amid the traffic on the other side of the Seine.

I sat there by myself and wondered which of my contradictory feelings would be in charge by the time she called that night.

Then I paid the bill and went to see her father.

⊞ **19** ⊞

ROBERT LEMAIRE HAD a solid five-floor house with recently sandblasted granite walls and large bay windows. Incised in the wall near the top of the polished oak entrance door was the name of an architect I'd never heard of and the date the house was built: 1865. A massive housekeeper in an apron opened the door. She had cynical eyes in a fat, motherly face.

I gave her my calling card. "I believe Monsieur Lemaire will be expecting me. If he's up."

"They're both up," she told me. "*She's* more up than he is, I'd say." She let me step into the entry hall and then shut the door firmly. It locked automatically. Only one lock. People who live on this side of the Parc Monceau don't worry much about robbery. The area has an abnormal number of cops and private cops to insure that they don't have to.

"Wait here," the housekeeper ordered. She went up a wide, curving stairway with my card, trudging the carpeted steps slowly and heavily. She vanished around a corner on the floor above.

A thick rug of rich, subtle colors covered much of the marble flooring in the entry. One mahogany wall had a collection of old blue-and-white Dutch tiles, mostly of naive angels in an odd assortment of poses. I studied some of them. One angel seemed to be doing a high dive into a lake. Another appeared to be having trouble balancing on a tightrope with an umbrella. Some artist centuries dead had left his sense of humor to the future.

A woman came strolling down the stairway. She was wearing a frothy black dress with thin shoulder straps and see-through layers of silk over opaque layers. She looked me in the eyes and smiled. I smiled back.

"You're the Pierre-Ange of the note Gabrielle left for Robert?" On French lips my name sounded fine. Especially on lips as luscious as hers.

She had to be Robert Lemaire's mistress. *One* of them, according to Gabrielle. She was about forty and definitely a luxury item.

If *she* had suggested dropping in to see me that night, I wouldn't have thought about reasons why it might not be a good idea. I knew that immediately: no reservations. Whether she was available or not didn't enter into that. Availability is not the essential ingredient for desire.

"Yes, I am," I told her. "And you're Robert Lemaire's friend."

"Friend? I don't know. . . . Playmate, yes. At the moment. Friend—time will tell."

We smiled at each other some more. I said, "What's your name?"

"Nora. Nora Darcy . . . If you're Gabrielle's latest, you are definitely an improvement."

"Latest what?"

"You *know* what I mean." Her look of appraisal was nothing like Gabrielle's. For one thing, it didn't make me nervous. I just let it soak in. Let her see whatever she could find there.

I said, "You don't think she's a bit too young for me?"

"The others have all been too young for her. Boys are all right for a woman my age. A girl her age needs a man.

Somebody in a couple has to know what they're doing, don't you think?"

"No."

"No?"

"I don't think two people belong together until each is complete, without need of further tuition."

"The optimum situation, naturally. Seldom happens." She shrugged a beautiful shoulder and said, "Robert is waiting for you. In the library. Up two flights and turn to your right."

I didn't want to part from her. "Is he recovered sufficiently to handle conversation?"

"If you don't talk too loudly. I'm afraid he didn't wind up having a very good time last night . . . this morning, actually."

"Did you?" It was crazy to feel jealousy this early in the game.

"Unlike Robert, I usually have the ability to make the best of any situation I'm foolish enough to get myself into."

"Accentuate the positive."

"What?"

"American song."

"It must be very new. I haven't heard it in the discos yet."

"It's very old. My grandfather liked to sing it. Nobody does anymore."

She eyed me with new curiosity. "You're American?"

"Half."

"Interesting." She continued to look at me for a beat and then walked past me to an entry closet. "I have to get back to my apartment and change. In this dress I look like something left over from the night before."

"You look marvelous."

She was opening the closet. She paused and looked back at me for a long moment. "Do you live in Paris?"

"Off and on."

"Where are you when you're off?"

I told her. We looked at each other a bit longer. Then she got a sable wrap and a beaded purse from the closet. Turning her back to me, she held the wrap out to one side and waited. I took longer than necessary in draping it over her shoulders.

She opened her purse and handed me a card with her name and phone number.

I put it in my wallet and gave her the card that had both of my numbers on it. She tucked it in her purse. Then she went out the entrance without a word.

I closed the door behind her and went up the steps to find Gabrielle's father.

"My brother's politics and prejudices," Robert Lemaire told me bitterly, "go back to the war. An attempt to justify our father's part in helping to create that nightmare. I think Jean-Louis would like to *re*-create it."

He wore a blue satin robe and had a red silk scarf around his gaunt neck. Robert Lemaire was fifty-eight but looked older that Saturday afternoon. There were ugly dark pouches under his bloodshot eyes, and his cheeks were caving in. His hands trembled and he sounded as if his vocal cords had been sandpapered.

He finished off a tall glass of fresh orange juice and poured himself more from an art deco pitcher with a black-and-turquoise glaze. I sipped the coffee he'd had his housekeeper bring for me.

"Jean-Louis always looked up to our father as a god," he rasped. "He still worships his memory."

"But not you."

Robert Lemaire thought about it. His eyes squeezed shut. Maybe a jolt of hangover. After a moment he opened them but kept them narrowed against the daylight. "I *respected* him—until I came back after the war and found out what he'd done during the Occupation. After that I loathed him—and myself, for being his son."

He swallowed more of the orange juice to clear his throat. "I still do," he said quietly.

We were on a small, shaded balcony outside his third-floor library, seated in cushioned cane chairs at a wrought-iron table with a thick porcelain top. Below us among the trees of Parc Monceau a tinkly waltz played from a tiny carousel carrying very small children around on a variety of gaily painted horses plus a diminutive fire engine and stagecoach. Between there and a candy and waffle stand, mothers and nannies were lining up with kids waiting for their turn to ride. On the other side was the statue of de Maupassant with a beautiful muse. She was holding one of his books but seemed more interested in the kids riding the merry-go-round.

"Your father was killed by a Jew," I said.

"Yes. By a man who had every reason to kill him."

"Would your brother approve of his son's joining a terrorist shooting of Jews? I'm talking about the one at the Rue des Rosiers a couple days ago."

"You think Henri was involved with that?"

"Yes, I do."

"My God, I hope not." Robert Lemaire drank more juice while he pondered my question. "No, Jean-Louis is much too cautious a man for that. He himself never makes any unprepared, hazardous moves. He concentrates on building his political power base one step at a time. Even for him, a return to our father's nightmare is very far in the future."

He shook his head. Carefully, but it still made him wince. "No, he would never countenance Henri's joining any group of terrorists. Most of all because the boy could get hurt himself doing so. Jean-Louis does love his son."

"I think Henri slipped the leash and did it anyway. I think your brother found out and is scared to death about it."

"I've *very* sorry to hear it." Gabrielle's father fell silent, looking down unhappily at the merry-go-round in the park.

It had stopped turning. A teen-age girl in patched jeans, a denim jacket, and a red cowboy hat was lifting children off and helping the new ones to climb on. When it was full, the carousel began turning again, its tinkly music resuming.

"When Henri moved to Paris," Robert Lemaire told me, "I made a point of dining with him from time to time. In an attempt to wean him away from Jean-Louis's dangerous leanings. I failed to be persuasive enough, I'm afraid. Like Jean-Louis, he looks up to his father too much. Whatever Jean-Louis believes is gospel for him."

"When did you see Henri last?"

"More than two months ago."

"He didn't mention any group he might have joined, any new contacts or friends?"

"No. He talked about going back to Reims in a year or so. To help his father in the business—and in politics. Like Jean-Louis, Henri looks forward to getting a government in power that will be completely on the side of big business against the unions and people he considers to be unjustly living off the taxes paid by big businesses. I reminded him that most of the businessmen who helped Hitler to power

for those same reasons ended up losing everything. But
Henri just smiled and ignored what I had to say.''

"He's stopped using his apartment. He's hiding out
someplace. Probably with his new friends. Do you know
any of them?''

"Not one, I'm sorry. I always met Henri alone. He
didn't mention anyone he was seeing in Paris.''

I took out a picture of Angelina Doniol and let him look
at it. "Do you know her?''

"I don't think so.''

"Her name's Angelina. She's the daughter of a German
named Reisler who settled in Reims after the war. She was
a language teacher in the Reims school your daughter and
Henri went to. Angelina Reisler—she married Leon Doniol, the son of a man who runs a souvenir shop across
from the Reims Cathedral.''

"I think I met Reisler once,'' Robert Lemaire said. "And
I knew Max Doniol. . . .'' He studied Angelina Doniol's
photograph again. "But I don't think I ever saw this girl.''

And that was that. I'd gotten some more background
information from Henri's uncle, but that was all.

I spent what was left of that Saturday afternoon showing
the pictures of Henri and Angelina around the brasserie
where Gabrielle's friend had seen them, at the Juarès Métro
end of Avenue Secretan. But I couldn't find anyone who
would acknowledge knowing them. I checked with Mussa
ben Zaer. He still didn't have anything for me. I told him
to concentrate on the area around the brasserie on Avenue
Secretan. There were people in that neighborhood who
wouldn't open up to me but would with Mussa.

It was getting toward dusk when I phoned Commissaire
Gojon, only to learn what I'd anticipated. Benito Santato

showed no sign of breaking down and telling anything useful. Gojon hadn't turned up any further leads elsewhere. I told him my luck matched his, and I drove back across the city toward Place Contrescarpe.

I parked my car in the garage two blocks away and headed for my apartment on foot. There was a very special phone call I wanted to make in privacy.

Detectives get into the habit of observing. You register whatever is going on in any street you drive through. You notice everybody who enters any restaurant you're eating in, and whom they talk to.

After years of that it becomes automatic. You are not even consciously aware that you're doing it, most of the time.

Until something clicks, and you tune into it.

It clicked when I was half a block from my apartment.

There was a gray Mercedes sedan I didn't recognize parked there illegally, with two wheels up on the pavement so other cars could squeeze past up the narrow street.

Its license number ended with 51.

The department number for the region around Reims is 51.

I looked around. Nobody was watching me. The entrance to my courtyard wasn't under surveillance.

That left my apartment. And maybe somebody waiting for me inside it.

⊠ 20 ⊠

APPROACHING BY WAY of the courtyard was out. Anyone watching from inside the front windows of my apartment would have an unobstructed view of the courtyard entrance. I walked halfway around the block to Rue Mouffetard. A covered alleyway ran between buildings there. I went through it into a dim little courtyard inside the heart of the block. Most of it was taken up by the big orange trash containers of the buildings around it. From there I turned left into another covered alleyway that led past the rear of the four-story house containing my apartment.

The rear wall had no windows. It was made of rough stone and was unusually thick. The only opening was a rear door that had been set in after breaking through the wall there sometime around the turn of the century. Like many of the buildings around Contrescarpe, the house was a melange of different centuries. The back had been a section of the ancient defense wall around Paris in the thirteenth century. Most of the house had been built against it between 1600 and 1700. The rest was the result of a renovation program after World War II.

I opened the back door and went in. Few doors of the apartment buildings in that neighborhood are kept locked. Security is left up to individual tenants. Halfway along the narrow hall that led from the rear to the front door I quietly climbed a flight of worn wooden steps.

There were two doors on the landing above: one to my

apartment, the other to Fritz Donhoff's. Each of us had keys to the other's apartment. I got out my key ring and used two of the keys to unlock Fritz's door, stepped inside, and relocked it.

Our adjacent apartments were laid out alike. All the rooms had high ceilings. The front room was spacious, and Fritz used his as a combination living room, library, and office, with a wide studio couch against one wall for any guest who wanted to sleep over.

I went through it into the big eat-in kitchen. After moving one of the chairs, I stood on it and pulled a top drawer of a cabinet all the way out. There was a concealed compartment behind it. I took out Fritz's compact model Beretta 92SB pistol. Reaching in again, I got its ammunition magazine, heavy with its full load of fourteen 9mm cartridges.

I got down off the chair, loaded the magazine into place inside the Beretta's black plastic grip, made sure I had a live round in the chamber, and snicked off the pistol's safety lever. The solid weight of the gun in my hand was comforting and familiar. I kept the same pistol in my own apartment, hidden in the living room.

I walked through a short corridor past the bathroom into Fritz's back bedroom. Taking some of his hanging suits and topcoats out of his closet, I draped them on his bed. Then I got down on my knees inside the closet.

In the back was the door we'd had installed in the wall between our bedrooms. You wouldn't spot it unless you knew it was there. It was covered with the same flowered wallpaper as the rest of the closet interior. With my left hand I opened the latch hidden under a flap of wallpaper near the floor.

Then I was looking into the darkness of my own closet.

Its door was closed, the way I'd left it. It had fewer clothes in it than Fritz's closet. I didn't live there that much anymore. I crawled through and stood up, holding the Beretta level in my right fist, and pushed my closet door all the way open with my left.

It opened without a sound, thanks to well-oiled hinges. My bedroom was empty. I'd been fairly sure it would be. The room had a side window, but it didn't look out at anything but a blank wall of the next building. I moved silently out of the bedroom, through the corridor past the bathroom, and into my eat-in kitchen.

From there I could see the man waiting for me in the living room.

He had pulled my leather-padded wing chair over near the front windows, where he could keep watch on the courtyard below while he waited. All I could see of him was wide shoulders sticking out on either side of the chair-back and a bull neck supporting a solid round head above it.

I said, "I'm aiming at the back of your fat neck. I want to see your hands above your head."

His hands jerked up into view. Big, heavy hands. "How did you come in?" He sounded surprised, but more curious than scared.

The voice was familiar.

I drifted around to one side, where I could see the face: Commissaire Emeric.

"Can I lower my hands now?" he asked evenly.

I rested a hip on the edge of the desk next to the front windows and put the Beretta down beside me, leaving my hand near it.

Emeric lowered his hands, resting them on the padded arms of the wing chair. "About time you got back."

I said, "Let me see your warrant to break into my apartment."

"I didn't break in," he told me innocently. "Take a look at your locks."

"So you brought a locksmith, or your own set of passkeys. If you don't have a warrant, it's still illegal entry."

"What are you talking about? I came here, rang your bell, you were home and asked me in. Like the polite type you are."

My word against that of a commissaire.

He glanced at his wristwatch. "A friend of mine is waiting nearby to have a word with you. At this point he's been waiting almost two hours."

"A friend with a Mercedes from Reims."

Emeric nodded. "Monsieur Jean-Louis Lemaire, whose time is more valuable than yours and mine. He's in that English pub at the end of the block, having tea with his chauffeur. Let's go out to his car, and I'll go get him."

"You can bring him up here."

"No, he wants to be sure it's a private talk."

"I don't have the apartment bugged."

"I'd have to bring in an expert to make sure of that. Come on, do it his way."

There was no reason not to.

I was waiting beside the Mercedes when Emeric came back with Jean-Louis Lemaire and the uniformed chauffeur. Lemaire got into the back seat and shut the door without a word or nod of greeting. He looked as if he was having difficulty controlling anger—or fright.

The chauffeur strolled on past. I went around the Mercedes and got in beside Lemaire. The chauffeur sat on the battered fender of a Volkswagen a few cars away and lit a cigarette. Emeric leaned against a near wall watching us, not close enough to hear what we said.

Lemaire started it without preamble, his voice tight. "I understand you're still searching for Henri."

I didn't have to ask if it was Emeric who had given him that information. "The one I'm searching for is a girl named Sarah Byrne. It's just that at the moment finding your son seems to be the best way to find her."

"I don't know where he is." He had told me that before, at the château. But this time it sounded different: a worried confession. "I can't find anybody who does know."

"It worries you."

He studied me. Then he said heavily, "I have reason to think Henri may have been seeing some . . . people I wouldn't approve of. I want to find him. And make certain he stops seeing them."

"You want me to help."

He studied me again, unsure. He was not a man who was used to that feeling. "If *you* happen to find him and bring him to me, I'll pay you twenty thousand francs."

The numbers had a persuasive weight of their own; even if you converted that sum to American dollars it would still come to more than two thousand.

"If you can see to it," Lemaire continued, "that Henri is not touched by any trouble associated with these people he's been seeing, I'll double that fee."

"That's a lot of money," I said.

"If you care to inquire, you'll learn that where money is concerned, I deliver whatever I promise."

"I'm sure of that." Big business can't be done any other way. If your word isn't good enough, you lose the ability to make quick deals before the competition gets in there.

If I delivered his son to him safe and sound, he *would*

deliver the fee. On the other hand, he couldn't be certain his promise would get me to do what he wanted. But it was a form of extra insurance. Emeric would have told him there was always a chance that I would be the one who found Henri first. If I did, Lemaire's offer would be there to nudge me into doing it their way. Emeric would also have told Lemaire about my reputation for liking money. Making the offer didn't lose him much, and it could gain him his son.

"Is it a deal?" Lemaire asked me.

I shrugged. "It's the best offer I've had for some time." That was true enough.

"You'll try to locate Henri for me?" he insisted. "Get him to me? No one else?"

"I can try," I said. "But if I'm going to help you, you have to help me do it. *Is* your son still in Paris?"

"I've told you, I don't *know* where he is."

"You do know he has Sarah Byrne with him, though."

Lemaire hesitated. "I know he was seeing an American girl of that name at one point. I don't know if he is still in touch with her. I never met her."

Probably true, but not much help. I asked him, "When was the last contact you had with your son?"

"When you were out there at the house. He phoned me."

"What about?"

"Just to say hello, nothing special."

"Was he calling from Paris?"

"I'm not sure."

"Where have you looked for him so far?"

"I haven't. Except for phoning some friends and asking if they've seen him. They haven't. *You* are my first attempt to get professional help in actually searching for him."

With Emeric standing there, that was obviously as untrue as his answers to my previous two questions. But then, I wasn't being honest with him, either. Perfect business relationship.

There was only one thing I could be sure of. He was scared. He had fed dark ideas to his son, and Henri had gone much further in acting them out than Jean-Louis Lemaire had ever intended. The possible consequences terrified him.

When I got out of the Mercedes, Emeric pushed himself away from the wall and came to meet me. "Is it a deal?"

"Seems to be."

"Good. You'll do much better for yourself cooperating with us than with Gojon. Have you gotten any new leads you haven't told him about yet?"

I nodded. "One of my journalists just tipped me that Henri was seen with some girl in Montparnasse last night. In one of those little bars in the street behind the Coupole."

Emeric let a little excitement show in his mean eyes. "I'll check it out."

So they really didn't have any idea where Henri was.

"You're already starting to earn that bonus," Emeric said. "Keep it up. Any new leads you get, you let *me* know from now on. First and fast. You only communicate with Monsieur Lemaire through me. And you don't tell Gojon *anything* more. Agreed?"

"Absolutely."

He signaled the chauffeur and climbed into the Mercedes with Lemaire. The chauffeur got in front and drove them away. I went back up to my apartment and phoned Gojon.

"Is this line safe?" I asked him, thinking of the spy Gojon thought Emeric had planted among his men.

"I'm having it checked twice a day, lately. You can talk. What have you got for me?"

I told him about my meeting with Emeric and Lemaire.

"You told them you'd go along with it."

"They may be under that impression."

"You really are a bastard."

"Now you know something you didn't before."

I hung up on him and then made the phone call that had been delayed by Emeric and Lemaire.

About nine o'clock that night the phone in my bedroom rang. It was Gabrielle. My day for the Lemaire family.

"Where are you?" I asked her.

"Still outside Paris. I'm sorry, but I don't think I'm going to be able to see you tonight."

"That's all right . . . ."

"I . . . I'm having a better time than I expected."

"With Joel."

"Yes. I don't know how long the feeling will last, but . . ."

"Accentuate the positive."

"What?"

"A saying I just made up. Have a good time."

I put the phone down on my bedside table and turned back to Nora. "Want to go out to eat?"

She said, "Mmmmm . . ." Then she said, "Later . . . I'm not up to putting all those clothes back on yet."

"My sentiments, exactly." I hadn't felt like this since Maidi had left. Judging by what holding Nora Darcy in my arms did to me, I was on my way back to normal.

* * *

The next day my search for Sarah Byrne, Henri Lemaire, and Angelina Doniol abruptly exploded into something much bigger.

⊠ 21 ⊠

SO MUCH OF Babette's beauty was in the strong bone structure of her face and the lively eyes that age would never be able to erase it. The years had cut deep lines in it, but it was still there. She was almost as tall as I and still had the build of an athletic Venus. Strong waist, long legs, wide hips, full bosom. Mother Earth.

"It's *Bébé!*" a former Minister of Defense cried when he saw her. "Bébé" had been her *nom de guerre* as a teenager in the Resistance.

We were just making our entrance under the massed chandeliers in the decaying nineteenth-century magnificence of the long and lofty Salle des Fêtes, at the rear of the Elysée Palace. The former minister left one of the groups of wartime Resistance leaders assembled there and marched over to us. Babette disengaged herself from my arm and he embraced her joyfully. It was like watching a scrawny spaniel trying to hug a full-grown lioness.

"I don't think it's fair," he told her. "I become a shrinking little old man and you remain a young goddess."

Babette bent her head to bestow three lusty kisses on his cheeks. "Old men are wonderful for a woman's ego. I don't know what I'll do when the last of you is dead."

One thing my mother is not is the soul of tact.

"Bébé," he chided her indulgently, "it is the height of impertinence to remind your elders that the grim reaper hovers. I take back saying you're a goddess. You are a naughty little girl.''

She blushed and dimpled and kissed him again. Babette wasn't the sort of woman who wants proof that men respect her. Her self-esteem was strong enough to require no bolstering. What my mother expected of the men she liked, she'd once explained, was what everybody, man or woman, really needed from the world around them: ''warm, affectionate cuddling.''

By then other friends from the Resistance were gathering nostalgically around her. The wives who'd accompanied some of them to the Elysée luncheon reception stood apart and watched and tried to appear amused by it.

''Where is Sylvia Vouret?'' Babette asked a retired admiral.

''She's not here yet,'' he told her, ''but she'll be coming. I talked to her by phone yesterday. She told me she would leave Brussels early this morning to be sure to make it.''

Sylvia Vouret was the current chief of France's delegation at the European Community's headquarters in Brussels, and also the EC's commissioner for foreign trade. She had long been one of my mother's best friends among the Resistance veterans. I'd known her since I was seven. Sylvia Vouret was tiny alongside Babette, but as tough as she was kind and funny. She had survived being captured and badly beaten by the Milice, the French paramilitary fascist organization that had operated in collaboration with the Gestapo and SS.

One of my early memories was of being with her and my mother in a restaurant when a loud belch had burst out of me before I could stop it. I'd gotten hot with shame, but Sylvia had put an arm around me and delivered what

I'd considered the wisest adult words I'd ever heard: "Better out in the big world than inside little you."

I'd had my first crush on her.

Babette was too occupied with her old buddies to require my presence any longer. I made my way to the long cocktail table set up by the tall windows overlooking the Elysée's back garden and asked for a large Bloody Mary. There are times when you need a drink that delivers a more immediate jolt than wine. Nora Darcy and I had gone to sleep late and wakened early to explore further permutations of carnal pleasure before I had gone to pick up Babette at noon. I downed a third of my Bloody Mary and gave the jolt time to grab hold. Then I nursed the rest and looked around the suffocating antique elegance of the biggest room in the palace.

One corner was roped off so none of the guests would endanger life and limb by wandering over there. The ornate ceiling was sagging alarmingly. They still hadn't succeeded in repairing the rotting roof above that section.

The Elysée Palace has a lot of problems like that. It's the official residence and executive base of the presidents of France, but none of them has liked living there. Their wives have all loathed it. The wife of the current one refused to sleep in it.

It's too big, too old, and you can't find craftsmen who know how to do work like they used to. Most of the interior decoration and furnishings date back to Madame de Pompadour. Recurrent attempts to modernize the place have only resulted in a jarring mix of nightclub-plastic-garish with the uncomfortable antiquity. The rooms are drafty, and the temperature of the steam heating system installed in the 1930s is impossible to regulate properly. De Gaulle

called the Elysée a big flytrap. Another president referred
to it as a golden prison.

The current president had escaped from it that Sunday.
Like most sensible Parisians affluent enough to do so, he
was spending part of the weekend in the country. He'd left
his prime minister to preside over this Resistance veterans'
get-together, aided by a number of assistant ministers.

I was having a fierce debate with two of them, the assistant ministers of Culture and Agriculture, when we were
all summoned into the Grand Salle à Manger for the lunch.

Sylvia Vouret still hadn't arrived.

We had finished the first course and were being served
the main course when we found out why.

One of the senior members of the Elysée's secretarial
staff entered the dining room, hurried over to the First Assistant Minister of the Interior, and whispered in his ear.
He excused himself and went off to the Salon Murat to take
a phone call. When he came back he looked stunned.

He held up both hands for silence, and when he got it
he told us grimly, "Sylvia Vouret was kidnapped this
morning as she was leaving her house in Brussels to take
a plane here. It was not known until less than an hour ago,
when a phone call was received by a television station in
Belgium. The caller announced that Madame Vouret is
being held hostage by some group calling itself the United
European Brigade. They promise to release her unharmed
if we will release a terrorist now under arrest in Paris in
connection with the attack at the Rue des Rosiers. A man
named Benito Santato."

He paused as though he was having difficulty with his
breathing. Then he finished. "The caller said that if Santa-

to is not freed, Sylvia Vouret will be . . . executed. That is all that I know at this point.''

In the roar of voices that filled the room when he stopped talking I only heard what one of them said as I got up to leave.

''Sylvia has experience at surviving captivity,'' Babette said beside me. ''She can do it again.''

But she didn't sound as sure of that as she wanted to.

⊠ 22 ⊠

BACK IN THE third century, it is said, Saint Denis tucked his head under his arm after it had been lopped off by unbelievers and carried it up over the Parisian hill now called Montmartre in honor of that miracle.

I carried a copy of Angelina Doniol's picture up the same hill to Gojon's apartment.

Which was a lot like handing him my head. Because I also told him everything else I had concerning Angelina Doniol. That had to include the fact that I'd had the picture since Friday. Admitting that was part of my penance. If I had given Gojon the photograph and information two days earlier, the police *might* have caught Angelina Doniol in time to prevent her gang from snatching Sylvia Vouret.

Not likely, since they'd shifted out of France into Belgium. But possible.

"We'll see how you look by the time this is all over," Gojon told me in a surprisingly subdued tone. "At that point we'll weigh how much you've fucked us up against how much you've helped us."

"And if the plus side isn't a good deal heavier than the negative you'll try to get my right to work in France canceled."

Gojon nodded. "I'll do my very best to. You can always go back to work in Chicago, I suppose. A very cold and windy city, so I've heard."

"Not always. Sometimes it's very hot and windy."

I'd phoned his office and been told that even commissaires had their days off. Gojon's apartment was too large for a man whose wife had left him. It was near the top of the hill. The big front room had windows on both sides. Those on one side looked toward Montmartre Cemetery, where romantics still came every Sunday to place her favorite flowers on the grave of the Lady of the Camellias. The other windows had a view of the steep stone steps that led all the way up to the church of Sacré-Coeur and all the way down to the city's greatest concentration of cheap street whores around place Pigalle.

Gojon made us instant coffee while we talked. He took his into another room to phone the office of his chief inspector. He was gone a long time. I sat in his front room and drank from my cup while I looked at the photographs we had spread out on the table.

Angelina Reisler Doniol. Henri Lemaire and the late Fernand Claudel. Benito Santato.

The picture of Sarah Byrne was on the table, too. If she was still alive, and still with them at this point, either she was their prisoner (in which case I needed all the help possible in locating her) or she was helping them (in which case I didn't want to do anything further to shield her).

"Are you still on the case?" I asked Gojon when he came back into the front room.

"As much of a case as we've still got, here in Paris. As of now it belongs more to the Belgian police. What you've told me confirms the fact that the terrorists of the Rue des Rosiers *are* members of this United European Brigade that's holding Sylvia Vouret hostage somewhere in Belgium." With infinite distaste, he repeated the name the group was calling itself. "The United European Brigade . . . united pieces of shit!"

"Kidnapping Sylvia Vouret can't have been done on the spur of the moment," I said. "They have to have been making plans about how to pull it off for some time. Before you arrested Santato. That just gave them another reason. They were here in Paris during most of that planning period. There are bound to be some loose threads left behind here."

"Sure," Gojon agreed absently. "And we'll find some of those threads—eventually. But eventually is no good any more. The Brussels police got a phone call half an hour ago. Apparently the same person who called the television station earlier. The terrorists have given us a deadline."

He stared out the windows in the direction of the cemetery. "This coming Friday. If we haven't let Santato go by then, they're going to chop off one of Sylvia Vouret's fingers. And another every day that we hold him after that. If we still haven't released him when all her fingers are gone, they'll kill her."

I took a couple of slow, deep breaths, but it didn't make the sickness go away. "Your government has given in to terrorist demands before," I reminded him thickly.

"Too often," he conceded. "Like America and almost every other western nation. That's why terrorists keep doing things like this. They don't try it against the Soviet Union, because they know it wouldn't work."

"I don't want a political lecture," I growled at him. My anger level had shot up with the announcement at the Elysée. Gojon's latest announcement had sent it higher.

"And I shouldn't be giving one," he agreed. "The thing is that right now government policy has switched to *not* giving in to ultimatums. Just a phase. In time they'll get over it and go back to falling to their knees under pressure. But maybe not in time to save Madame Vouret."

"Was the one who made the calls in Brussels a woman?"

"A man."

Not Angelina Doniol.

"With a strong German accent."

Not Henri Lemaire, either.

Gojon said, "I have to change and get to my office. And arrange to have all the information we've got sent to Brussels." He gestured at the table. "Along with these pictures."

I thought about the Sylvia Vouret I'd known since I was a kid—and about what they were threatening to do to her. "Anything more I find out," I told him as I got up to leave, "I'll pass on to you immediately."

"I'm sure you will," he said dryly. "From now on. At this point you need as many favorable items in my book as you can manage. They'll have to be *very* favorable to make up for the rest."

I went down the slope of Montmartre and turned left into the Arab neighborhood for another talk with Mussa ben Zaer.

He told me that a waiter at the brasserie on Avenue Secretan thought he'd seen a woman who looked like Angelina Doniol's picture. She had been in the place a few times to eat. Once with a man who *might* have been Henri Lemaire. Another time with a different man. The waiter didn't know anything more about her or about either of the men.

Mussa hadn't turned up anybody else who recognized the people in the photographs I'd given him.

"If she ate three times we know of in that brasserie," I told him, "she must have lived somewhere not far from it.

Keep trying around that area. I'll owe you another big favor if you get me something more.''

I slipped Mussa one of the copies of Santato's picture that Gojon had given me and asked him to show that one around, too.

Then I drove back to my apartment to see if there were any messages on the answering machine from Fritz Donhoff in Germany.

I didn't have to check the machine. Fritz was waiting for me, stretched out on the sofa in my living room fully dressed but sound asleep.

23

"IT HAS BEEN a tiring few days," Fritz told me. "After you phoned me Friday I spent that evening and much of the night seeing various contacts in Munich. Up early Saturday morning to collect that photograph from your Lufthansa stewardess at the airport. Then on to Stuttgart for most of Saturday. Up to Hamburg that evening, and another late night. Down to Frankfurt this morning."

He was sitting across from me in my kitchen, drinking the vervain tea I'd prepared for him. I'd offered to make him strong coffee, but he didn't want his nerves jagged up. "I intend to have a small early dinner and go right to bed. I need at least ten hours of sleep to put me right."

Fritz did look weary. He always had big bags under his eyes, but they didn't usually have that dark sag. He didn't look rumpled, however, not even after napping on my couch. He'd combed his glossy white hair and smoothed the wrinkles out of his velvet suit, made sure the necktie with its opal stickpin and cuffs with their pearl cuff links were just so. The old-fashioned dandy attire never looked silly on him. Fritz was an impressive man: tall, strong, heavy, radiating calm, competence, and dignity.

I said, "Sounds like you saw every police contact you've got in Germany."

"Only some of them. And a number of other people they suggested I talk to. Former left-wing extremists who have become disillusioned with terrorism. Ones who have settled down to being leftists who prefer achieving their ends through lawful means.''

''Happens with most of them. That's why you've got so few extremists who're much over thirty. By then most of their causes have let them down. The only ones who won't admit it to themselves are the fanatics.''

Fritz nodded. ''The pathologically violent.'' He sipped tea from the large mug I'd filled for him. ''Martin Droscher was one of those. You'll remember I told you the name sounded familiar when you gave it to me over the phone. Droscher was once a member of the Baader-Meinhof gang. Sometime after that group was broken up Droscher was caught by the police. They finally had to let him go because they couldn't put together the sort of evidence against him that would stand up in court. He left Germany for a time after that. When he returned, he was with a woman whom some people recognize from your photograph of Angelina Doniol. In Germany she called herself Angelika Reisler.''

''Reisler was her maiden name.''

''And Angelika is a German variant of Angelina. She helped Droscher organize his own terrorist group. Some say that he was only the titular head of it—that she was the real leader. Much like Ulrike Meinhof and Andreas Baader. They pulled some bank holdups to get funds for their gang. Two innocent bystanders were killed in the first. In the second, Droscher was killed by the police. They had been tipped off by a defector from the gang. After that our Angelina-Angelika took over as sole leader of what was left of that group and began recruiting new members.''

Fritz tasted his tea and frowned at me. ''It's getting cold.''

I got up to brew him some more.

''One of her new recruits was a girl named Gudrun

Sturm. I spoke to her at length in Hamburg. She had fled there after quitting the gang, going into hiding and living in considerable fear until she learned Angelina was no longer in Germany. Two other defectors from the gang had been found murdered. Gudrun is certain that Angelina killed them—as a method of discouraging further desertions."

I refilled Fritz's mug with tea hot enough to scald my mouth. But he tried it and said, "That's better. Exactly right."

He drank some more before continuing. "Gudrun originally joined the gang because her lover was in it. She quit after she realized that he was more in love with Angelina-Angelika than with her. That seems to have been one of Angelina's recruiting methods. Young men, and some women, would become infatuated with her, drawn to her domineering character. She encouraged them to have affairs with outsiders in order to pull in more recruits."

I thought about Henri Lemaire romancing Sarah Byrne, though he was already hooked on Angelina Doniol.

"It became increasingly difficult, about that time, for *any* of the fanatic groups in Germany to get new recruits. The growing efficiency of the police campaign against terrorism there began scaring off potential members. Angelina's small group became even smaller as a result of angry disagreements over her radical proposals for remedying that problem. One of her ideas was to attract terrorists who had been forced to flee from other countries. To make her group truly international."

"The United European Brigade."

"Yes. Another of her notions was to recruit hardened criminals recently released from prisons. She thought they would be ideal: men already outside bourgeois society, with experience in evading and attacking it. But what really went against the grain for most in her group, especially its staunchest communists, was her third proposal. To recruit from the extreme *right* as well as the far left.

"Her point there was that, as she put it, at this stage the motives and methods of both are identical. To create enough random violence to make people sick of ineffectual democratic-capitalist governments unable to protect their citizens. Angelina was prepared to make certain concessions to bring neo-Nazi recruits into the group. Others were not, and they split away from her.

"Only two stuck with her. One is a German named Kurt Seidel. A hardened criminal with a long record of armed robbery and assaults. He's spent half his life in various prisons." Fritz took out a photograph and put it on the table.

The face that looked out of it was brutal. Thick, dark eyebrows sticking out of a prominent ridge of bone over squinty eyes. Caved-in nose. Thin, contemptuous mouth.

"The other who stuck with her," Fritz said, "is a former member of the Italian Brigades Rouge."

"Benito Santato."

"Yes. Seidel and Santato—it sounds like one of those old vaudeville teams, doesn't it?"

"But not a funny one."

"No. A deadly nucleus for the formation of a new gang. But not in Germany. Angelina was afraid of the ones who'd broken away from her there. Afraid they might betray her to the German police. With reason, if Gudrun's suspicion that she murdered two defectors is true."

"So she comes to France with Seidel and Santato to build a new group. The crazy mixture she was after. Neo-Nazis—that would fit Henri Lemaire."

"If he was already smitten with her when younger, that

would make it easier for her to persuade him to join her. I'm told she is still extremely attractive to men. Especially the sort who fasten on to stronger personalities."

The things Fritz had told me explained some of the peculiarities I'd been running into. "A merger of fanatics of the right and fanatics of the left and hard-core criminals. It's weird."

"Not entirely," Fritz said judiciously. "You start with people going after the power to achieve quite different objectives. After a time they are simply going after the power. Since the power they all want is the same, and so is their method of reaching for that power, it finally brings them together."

"Achieving power requires getting people to follow you," I said. "The attack in the Rue des Rosiers could have been Angelina Doniol's way of proving to Henri and any other neo-Nazis in her group that their purposes *are* the same, at this point."

"Probably. Also, for her to keep those people and attract others she has to prove she'll stick by them if they get in trouble. Therefore the kidnapping of Sylvia Vouret, in retaliation for the arrest of Benito Santato."

I nodded. "You've done a good job, Fritz. Thank you." He *always* did a good job, and he didn't need me to tell him that he had done it again, but Fritz believed in those little spoken courtesies.

He nodded gravely in appreciation of my tribute to his skill and dedication.

I told him what I'd told Gojon about the loose threads Angelina Doniol's gang must have left behind them somewhere in Paris.

"It occurs to me," I said, "that if she's been pulling

professional criminals into her group, that's one area where nobody's dug too deeply for those threads so far. You know a lot of people in the Paris underworld.''

"So do you."

"Yes, but not as many as you do. And not as well as you know them—going all the way back to the war.''

He had been a police detective in Munich until the Nazis had taken power there. They didn't like the things Fritz had been saying about them and their Führer. He fled to Paris, and when the Nazis took over there he sank into the underground. He'd met a different kind of Resistance fighter there than I'd seen earlier that day at the Elysée. Many were criminals, from petty crooks to professional killers.

Some French criminals helped the Nazis, who found their services useful and paid well. But others joined the Resistance for one reason or another. Among them Fritz acquired a very special respect. By the end of the Occupation he was believed to have murdered more Nazi officials and French collaborators than any other single person.

"I'm thinking especially of the ones you knew who were in the business of illegal buying and selling of weapons. On a small scale. Some of them are still in business, or know people who are. Angelina's United European Brigade had to get its arms from somebody.''

"Excellent thought," Fritz told me. "I'll get on it. Tomorrow. At the moment I am going to have a light dinner and go to sleep. I don't want to be disturbed until the morning.''

He stood up. "Thank you for the herb tea. It was delicious, and most relaxing.''

"You're very welcome," I assured him.

He nodded gravely and trudged off to his own apartment.

* * *

Early Monday morning I made copies of the picture of Kurt Seidel and took one to Commissaire Gojon. Fritz Donhoff began canvassing his underworld friends with copies of it and of the other photographs I'd collected. I started passing out copies among my own acquaintances in the underworld. Neither of us turned up even a hint of a lead that day. I phoned Gojon in the afternoon and again that evening. He didn't have anything new, either.

But shortly after nine that night, Mussa ben Zaer did.

Angelina had lived for a few weeks, recently, in a rooming house a short walk south of the brasserie where she'd been seen several times. She'd been using a false name, but the owner of the house was certain she was the woman in the picture of Angelina Doniol.

I got over there fast. The house was a shabby one behind the trees and park benches of the Quai de la Loire on one side of the Saint Martin canal. The owner told me he didn't know how she spent her time away from the house. She paid two weeks' rent in advance for her room and used it alone. Nobody ever came to visit her there, and the owner had never seen her being met by anyone when she went out.

"She *might* have had somebody she stayed with someplace else sometimes," the owner of the house said. "There were two or three nights she didn't come back here to sleep in her room."

"When did she move out of here?"

"Last Thursday. Late afternoon."

That was the same evening she had helped Henri Lemaire and Sarah Byrne move out of his apartment. I didn't learn anything that gave me a lead to where they might have moved.

I phoned Gojon again and told him what I'd come up with. He wasn't impressed, and I couldn't blame him.

"I understand you're trying your best to square yourself with me," he said. "But that's last week's news, of no use at all right now. You're wasting your time, Sawyer. If you really want to help, why don't you get yourself up to Brussels and see what you can find out there?"

It was a thought. The trouble was, I didn't know enough people in Brussels to do anything the Belgian police weren't already doing to find Sylvia Vouret and the terrorists who had her.

Tuesday morning Fritz and I went our separate ways to comb our underworld connections again. By noon we hadn't done any better than the day before. I put in a call to Gojon to see if *he'd* gotten anything new that morning. He had: news about Sylvia Vouret—from further away than Belgium.

"Last night an envelope was left with the night receptionist of a newspaper in Amsterdam. The receptionist's description of the man who left it fits the picture you gave me of that German ex-con."

"Kurt Seidel."

"Right. The envelope wasn't opened until early this morning, when the editor it was addressed to got in to work. It contained a Polaroid photograph of Sylvia Vouret. Sitting against what looks like a plain wooden fence or wall, holding last evening's edition of that Dutch newspaper."

"They've moved her all the way up to Holland?"

"Probably immediately after they kidnapped her, judging from the timing. There's a message with the photograph. Signed by the 'United European Brigade.' They want Santato put on a plane to Libya. They'll phone there Friday at noon. If Santato isn't there to talk to them by then, they'll start carrying out their threat about cutting off Sylvia Vouret's fingers and then killing her.''

"What's the French government's present position?''

"Not good, for Madame Vouret. They *won't* let Santato go.''

"Jesus . . .''

Gojon was silent for a moment. "I have some more bad news for you.'' He paused again.

"Tell me.''

"Sarah Byrne. She's dead.''

🔳 **24** 🔳

"SHE FELL FROM the roof of an abandoned warehouse slated for demolition, between the railroad embankment and the Bassin de la Villette," Gojon told me. "Fell, or was pushed."

"They killed her." My voice sounded toneless and far off, not part of me.

"Maybe. Impossible to tell. Her skull was smashed. That could be from the fall. Or part of it could have been done before she was thrown off. *If* she was thrown off."

I was sure of it. Angelina Doniol had killed two others who had quit her gang. How deeply Sarah had become part of that gang, I couldn't know. She'd gone along with them at least partway, out of her feelings for Henri and maybe out of excitement at what he chose to tell her about its plans. But then she'd learned the full extent of what they'd done and what they were planning—and had balked. They couldn't just let her walk off with what she'd known by then. . . .

"When did it happen?" I asked Gojon.

"Her body was found Saturday morning. She's been in the morgue up there since. There was no identification on her. It wasn't until today that her fingerprints got matched against the ones of Sarah Byrne I got from the FBI."

I seemed to be putting a lot of my strength into holding on to the phone. There was a taste of bile in my mouth.

Gojon was saying, "There's evidence that squatters have

lived inside that warehouse recently. But they're gone now. Nobody's been turned up yet who knows who they were or if the dead girl was one of them. Most of the buildings in that area are empty. Boarded up, waiting to be torn down.''

I walked into the nearest bar and downed two double whiskeys, one right after the other. Then I ordered a third.

Was I in some way responsible for the girl's death?

No. It was groundless self-flagellation to load that kind of guilt on myself. But . . .

Could I have done something different that would have saved her from dying?

Probably, *if* I had understood what was going on soon enough. I could have grabbed Sarah Byrne the instant I'd seen her and dragged her out into the street, shouting for the police. Or I could have approached Henri's apartment building more warily, with a gun ready.

But all the *could haves* were pointless. I also could have gotten there a few minutes later, and they would have been gone by then and I would never have seen Sarah Byrne at all. . . .

It was hard to think straight. My brain was numb. My stomach was ice. My heart thudded sickeningly.

I was on my fourth double when I stopped myself.

I was too French to indulge any further in that all-American malady of feeling responsible for everything bad that happened in the world.

Sarah Byrne, a dumb kid from California, had come to Paris and fallen for the wrong guy—and she was dead. Nothing I or anyone else could do would change that.

But Sylvia Vouret, whom I'd known since I was seven, was still alive. And perhaps still unharmed. At least until Friday.

It was now Tuesday.

I ordered a large cup of extra-strong black coffee and drank it down without stopping. Then I just made it into the toilet before I threw up.

I stayed in the bathroom for some time, running cold water over my hands and face and the back of my neck. Finally I returned to the bar and drank two thick espressos with enough caffeine to jolt my brain loose from my skull.

And began to think again.

I tried it on Fritz Donhoff: "*Why* would they make a point of letting us know where they are?"

"You mean because that's where they're not?" Fritz nodded thoughtfully. "Dutch papers *can* be purchased in Belgium shortly after they come out in Holland."

He thought about it some more, aloud. "They take a picture of Madame Vouret—in or near Brussels—holding the evening edition of that Dutch newspaper. One of Angelina's group, probably Kurt Seidel, takes the half-hour flight to Amsterdam and leaves it there. To concentrate the search for them up in Holland. While they remain hidden with Sylvia Vouret in Belgium. Definitely possible."

"Try another possibility," I said. "It starts the same way. Seidel flies the picture from Brussels to Amsterdam. Concentrating the hunt for Sylvia Vouret to the north of Belgium. Making it safer for Angelina Doniol's group to move her out of Belgium in the opposite direction. South— to Paris."

Fritz's frown was dubious. "Why would they do that?" He made it sound like an examination question. "Much safer for them to keep her inside Belgium's borders than to try shifting across in *any* direction."

"Maybe they don't have contacts they trust that much

inside Belgium. Don't know a hiding place where they'd feel secure in for a longish period."

"That could be," Fritz granted. He still looked dubious. "But any attempt to move their hostage across a border would involve other risks. You have customs officers doing spot checks of cars and trucks at every frontier control station—even in normal times."

I said, "Bear with me while I try to explain my reasoning."

Fritz laced his plump, powerful hands together across his vast chest and bore with me.

I held up a finger. "First of all, Angelina moved out of her rooming house on Thursday, and Henri left his apartment with Sarah Byrne the same day. But they stayed in Paris until at least late Friday night or early Saturday morning. Because that's when Sarah Byrne was killed. At some time not too long ago, Angelina must have gone up to Brussels with some of her group to work out how to kidnap Sylvia Vouret. Maybe a couple of them stayed up there. But lately, during the period when she would have been making arrangements for what to do *after* the snatch, Angelina Doniol has been here in Paris—not in Belgium, not in Holland."

"As far as you *know*," Fritz pointed out. "You can't account for all her time over the past few weeks."

"What we know is all we've got to work with," I snapped at him. "We can't work with what we *don't* know." I altered my tone quickly. "I'm sorry, Fritz."

"That's all right," he said graciously. "Your tension is understandable under the circumstances."

"Thank you." I held up another finger. "Secondly, the brasserie where Angelina Doniol was seen a number of times is a one-minute walk from the lower lock of the barge canal system's Port Number Two. And she rented a room for two weeks close to the Saint Martin canal. *And* Sarah Byrne's body was found not far from the barge basin of La Villette.''

"I see. . . . You're not thinking of the gang trying to smuggle Madame Vouret out of Belgium by road. You're thinking of them using a barge.''

"What do *you* think of it?''

"That it is an interesting thought," Fritz admitted slowly.

A tremendous amount of cargo is moved between European countries via their connecting networks of rivers and canals. Usually barges pass across frontiers with virtually no checking of their cargoes. A detailed inspection of any one barge would leave dozens more stalled behind it for hours. Any attempt to carry out spot checks on barges entering a country would cause a canal blockage in its neighboring country, stretching back for miles and lasting for days. That in turn would bring howls of indignation from businesses, unions, and officials of the European Community.

That was why some of Europe's smugglers liked to hide illicit merchandise among the legal cargoes of barges whenever they could find barge people willing to cooperate with them.

"Interesting," Fritz repeated. "But not much more solid than a calculated hunch. As I'm sure you realize.''

"Look at it this way," I told him. "If Angelina Doniol's gang has Sylvia Vouret up in Belgium, or Holland, there's not much we can do to help find her. Not in the little time that's left. *If* I'm right, maybe we can.''

We spent the rest of Tuesday asking our underworld contacts to concentrate on showing our collections of photographs to any smugglers they knew who had ever used the canals to move their stuff. We kept at it late into that night. And all through the next day.

IT WAS A small general merchandise warehouse overlooking the intersection where the canal of Saint Denis flows into the Ourcq canal up near the Porte de la Villete. An industrial section, quiet and almost deserted late at night. Not entirely deserted: the man who ran the canal warehouse had a little apartment above it.

"The first I ever saw her was about three weeks ago," he said. His name was Felicien Charcot and he was having difficulty dealing with his anxiety. "She was introduced to me by a guy I know and trust—*used* to trust."

"Who is he?"

Charcot shrugged. "Just a guy. I know him from years back, when we were both serving some time in Melun Prison." He gazed bitterly at the photograph of Angelina Doniol that lay on his threadbare purple satin tablecloth.

All of his living room was furnished like that—with what looked like auctioned items salvaged from a 1930s brothel. Fritz sat in a moth-eaten red plush armchair and smiled at the warehouse manager. I stood scowling by a gilt-framed painting of a lustful octopus doing unlikely things to a delighted mermaid.

Charcot's worry was not unwarranted, but neither was my impatience. It was nearly midnight. In less than half an hour Wednesday night would turn into Thursday morning.

"I want the *name* of the man who introduced you to her," I growled at him. "It might help us."

The man who had brought us there, Augustin Sauval, said to Charcot, "*Tell* them." He said it without turning around to look in our direction.

Sauval was standing at a window with his back to us, looking down through yellowed lace curtains at his car, parked between Fritz's and mine in the dark street below. Constant vigilance is one price of staying alive in his trade. Small-time illegal arms dealers occasionally get shot in Europe. More often they get blown up when they try to start their cars. Sometimes it's done by crooks who want to hijack their goods. Or by other dealers, to eliminate competition. But usually it's the work of professional assassins working for government intelligence departments that don't like some of the people a dealer is selling to.

Sauval had known Fritz since he was a kid, back when his father ran the little family arms business. Then Pop had gotten too old for it, and his son had carried on for him. It's encouraging that there are still some young people around with that kind of respect for their parents and tradition.

Charcot glared at Sauval's back. "I wish I'd never told *you* I knew her when you showed me that damned picture."

"Don't worry," Sauval said, continuing to watch his car. "Monsieur Donhoff will see you don't get into trouble because of it. If you give him everything you know."

"Indeed I will," Fritz assured Charcot soothingly. He can be one of the most soothing people I know. "On the other hand," he said, still smiling benignly, "if you *don't* help us I'll throw you to the cops. I imagine they will chew you up into very small and bloody pieces."

Charcot began to wilt, visibly. "I swear I didn't know it had anything to do with a kidnapping or terrorists when she made me the proposition. And I still didn't know when she took delivery. I thought it was just the usual: some kind of merchandise. I'd *never* have gone along with it if I'd guessed they were moving a *person*!"

I said, "Telling us what we want to know will prove that. Holding anything back proves you're lying."

"What the hell, I don't owe the guy any loyalty. *He* wasn't square with me when he brought this girl around to talk to me. He never let on what was really going on."

"His *name*," I repeated.

"Louis Roy," Charcot told me. "He beats people up for money. Or used to, before he joined up with *her*." He looked again at Angelina Doniol's picture.

Fritz said, "You think he's part of her group."

"I don't know anything about any group she's got. But he *was* taking orders from her and acting like he didn't mind. I used to think Roy was a real hard one. But she has him under her thumb; that's sure."

"What was her proposition to you?"

"A good chunk of money," Charcot said, "for helping them smuggle a large packing case from Belgium to here. Some cash up front, the rest when the case arrived."

"Did she say when she wanted it done?"

"She asked when I could do it. Well, I'd already set something up with a barge skipper who sometimes cooperates with me, for a percentage. He was bringing other stuff for me, from Antwerp. Due to arrive last night. She said that was fine with her."

It was what I'd thought. Angelina Doniol had planned the kidnapping of Sylvia Vouret well before Santato was caught. His arrest had only caused her to substitute the demand for his release for whatever ultimatum she'd originally planned.

"When did this barge leave Antwerp?" I asked Charcot.

"The night before last. Monday night."

Shortly after they took the photograph of Sylvia Vouret and it was flown to Amsterdam by Kurt Seidel.

"And it got in here last night," Fritz said. "When?"

"Late. Happens a lot, like I warned her and Louis Roy. It came in after two in the morning. I don't pay overtime, so I had to wait until next morning to unload the barge. Except for that packing case. *She* was here waiting for that. With Louis Roy and some other guy I don't know."

I put my other photographs next to Angelina Doniol's. Charcot pointed to Kurt Seidel's. "That's him."

Then he pointed to the picture of Henri Lemaire. "*He* came along on the barge from Antwerp, with the case. Passing as skipper's helper. He and Louis Roy and the other guy carried the packing case to the van they had waiting. She gave me what she'd promised and got in the back of the van with the young guy and the case. Then they went off with Louis Roy driving and this other guy in front beside him. And that's all I can tell you. I don't know anything else."

I said, "You didn't hear any sounds from inside the packing case."

"No. Absolutely nothing. I swear it."

Probably true. They would have shot Sylvia Vouret full of dope before loading the case on the barge to make sure of that.

Fritz said, "Describe the case."

"Nothing unusual. Made out of thick planks of wood. Solid. Big enough to hold a refrigerator."

"Describe the van they used."

"Ordinary little van. But big enough to hold the packing case. Fiat, I think. The kind lots of little businesses use."

"You didn't notice any business name on this one?" Fritz asked gently, fastening his baggy eyes on Charcot's face. "Nor the license number?"

Charcot hesitated. He looked at Sauval's back. Then at me. And then, for a longer time, at Fritz again. "Not the number . . . but the name. It was a funny one, so it stuck in my head: Saint Elvis and Company."

I asked for his commercial phone book. He got it and I opened it on the table. Fritz took his monocle from his breast pocket and screwed it onto his right eye so he could read the small print with me.

There were two different numbers and addresses listed for "Saint Elvis & Co." One was a residence in the Latin Quarter. The other was a shop in the Marché aux Puces, the main flea market of Paris.

"You take the residence," I told Fritz. "I'll try the flea market."

⊠ **26** ⊠

IT IS SAID to be the biggest thing of its kind in the western world. More than seventy acres of narrow streets and narrower alleys and passageways cutting between crowded rows of attached shops. At last count the number of shops came to some three thousand.

Just beyond the Porte de Clignancourt, the vast maze of the Marché aux Puces sprawls between the seedy suburbs of Saint Ouen and Saint Denis. They still call it a flea market, but nobody can remember the last time even a flush American tourist bought anything there without flinching at the price before giving in to temptation.

I parked my car just outside it, under an off-ramp of the elevated expressway that follows the city limits around Paris. I got a flashlight and crowbar out of the storage compartment and the small Mauser pistol from its hiding place inside the rear seat. This was one of those times when a situation justified the risk of being arrested with it on me.

I stuck the gun in the back of my belt, under my jacket, before entering the labyrinth of the market.

I kept to darkly shadowed alleys and passages as I threaded my way deeper into the market. When I had to cross a street, I looked and listened first. The night watchmen usually prowled in cars, cruising the streets and only pausing to glance into the alleys they passed. Anybody coming in with robbery in mind would have to use some kind of vehicle to carry out enough to make it worthwhile.

The Marché aux Puces does business only on Saturdays, Sundays, and Mondays. The rest of the week it is lifeless. Everything is locked up tight. Nothing moves in it except an occasional truck or van delivering goods to someone who has opened his place just long enough to take it in.

This late at night, in the middle of the week, the shops around me were dark, silent tombs in an endless cemetery.

Most of the shops I passed between were the size of two-car garages. But there were some that weren't big enough to hold one four-door sedan. Each was sealed tight by a wide steel roll-down shutter that covered the entire shopfront. Few had windows.

There are seven different sections inside the Marché aux Puces, each with its own name and specialties. Saint Elvis & Co. was listed as being in Alley #9 of the Vernaison section. When I reached the street that ran past it, I stopped dead and stared at its name.

I had forgotten there was another Rue des Rosiers here in the flea market.

Instant question: How did its being here connect with the attack on the other one, in the Marais? A question to be pondered later. I switched the Mauser to the front of my belt before crossing this Rue des Rosiers and entering the passageways of the Vernaison market.

The passages there were numbered according to a logic that escaped me. Alley #2 led into Alley #4. I found Alley #9 by going through Alley #1.

Saint Elvis & Co. was there, sandwiched between two other shops. Its steel roll-down shutter was closed and secured by a large padlock at the bottom. I stood close to it and listened but couldn't hear anything inside. Going along the short alley and turning into the next, I circled, searching for a window to the shop. There was none. Saint Elvis

& Co. backed against the rear wall of another shop. I returned to the front and listened again, this time for outside noises.

There was no car moving along the street outside this section, no one approaching on foot inside it.

Crouching, I used the crowbar to break open the padlock. I stuck the crowbar in my belt and took out the Mauser. With the pistol gripped in my right hand, I used the hand holding the flashlight to raise the shutter. Just high enough to duck inside under it.

Still crouched, I executed a fast, crablike side shift as I snapped the flashlight on, ready to fire the Mauser at anything that threatened.

Nothing did. Nobody was there. I rolled the shutter back down so my light couldn't be seen from outside and straightened up.

The shop was full of movie and pop music memorabilia. Old posters and vintage records. Photographs of stars and stills from films. Stacks of fan magazines. Plastic models of characters from *Star Wars* and other fantasy films. T-shirts adorned with pictures of Michael Jackson and James Dean. Behind the counter, the place of honor was taken by a framed oil painting of Elvis Presley, over a sign bearing the name of the shop and of its proprietor, Jean-Luc Renzo. Flanking Elvis and the sign were posters of *The Rocky Horror Picture Show* and of Arnold Schwarzenegger stripped to a loincloth to play Conan.

On my side of the counter stood a wooden packing case large enough to hold a refrigerator.

One of its sides had been pried open and leaned against the counter. It was empty.

I searched the place but couldn't find any indication that Angelina Doniol's terrorists had ever been there. Nor any evidence that it was Sylvia Vouret that had been removed from the packing case.

Returning to the case, I went down on one knee inside it and used the flashlight for a detailed inspection of its inner surface. There were small airholes near the top of the back. I kept searching. It took me almost five minutes to spot it: little scratches down near the bottom.

I shined the flash on the scratches, angled from one side, and ran my fingertips over them to confirm by feel. Two letters had been gouged into the wood, probably by a fingernail.

The initials "S.V."

As Babette had said, Sylvia Vouret had experience at being a captive. She must have done it before the injection of drugs had put her all the way out. Or when it was wearing off, before they removed her from the box.

I was getting out when the phone on the counter rang, jarring my nerves.

It rang a second time and then stopped. I put my hand on the phone and waited, counting silently. Twenty seconds . . . then it started ringing again. I snatched it up and said, "Yes . . ."

Fritz's voice came through. "I've been watching the apartment of Jean-Luc Renzo from my car. Nobody was there when I arrived. He showed up a minute ago, alone, in a car that he parked in front of the building before going up to his apartment. His business van is also parked there. Saint Elvis and Company. I had a look inside it before Renzo came home. Nothing at all in it of interest to us. Have *you* found anything?"

I told him what I'd found.

He said, "I'll phone Commissaire Gojon and tell him."

"Get him here fast."

"Yes. Together with Monsieur Renzo."

⊠ 27 ⊠

WHILE I WAITED I pondered logistics.

It must have been around three in the morning by the time Angelina Doniol and her three men had off-loaded the packing case containing their prisoner from the barge and gotten it into the van.

Then they had driven here with it.

The shop was only a way station, used to transfer Sylvia Vouret. They'd needed the van because it was big enough to carry the packing case, and a car wouldn't be. Once they opened the box and took her out of it, there inside the shop, they could shift her to a normal car and drive off someplace else with her.

Either the owner of Saint Elvis & Co. was with them at the time or he'd given them a note authorizing their use of his van and shop to show to the night watchmen who were bound to see them driving in and out of the Marché aux Puces at night.

I was left with a number of unanswered questions. The most important was: Where had they taken Sylvia Vouret from here?

I was still pondering that one when the steel shutter was rolled all the way up with a loud clang, and Commissaire Gojon stepped inside with Fritz Donhoff.

Behind them were two of Gojon's Brigade d'Intervention inspectors. Big young bruisers with at least one other shared qualification: Gojon must be sure neither was Emeric's spy.

They had the shop's proprietor, Jean-Luc Renzo, squeezed between them. He was a short, plump man in his thirties. His jacket and trousers were of soft, supple black leather, with hardly any shine. His belt was a slim chain with a padlock for its buckle. Even his high-heeled boots didn't raise his head above shoulder level of the young inspectors flanking him. His hair was colored gold and purple. At least he didn't have a safety pin stuck in his earlobe. Just a plain gold earring, like a wedding band.

Gojon took the flashlight from me without a word and kneeled inside the packing case to see for himself.

"I still don't understand this," Jean-Luc Renzo quavered, making an unsuccessful try at indignation. He wasn't going to be as hard to crack as Benito Santato. He stabbed a finger at me. "*This* man has broken into my shop. Why aren't you taking *him* into custody instead of me?"

One of the inspectors looked down at him and said politely, "You're not in custody, Monsieur Renzo. Not yet, anyway."

Gojon climbed out of the packing case and stood up. "*Now* he is," he said. He'd found the S.V. initials. "Put handcuffs on him. Behind his back. *Tight*."

Gojon didn't take Jean-Luc Renzo to his office. He didn't want Emeric alerted.

A few block above Gobelins, the oldest and most famous tapestry factory in France, on the avenue named for it, there was a building that had been boarded up for years while it waited for someone to get around to either renovating it or tearing it down. The pair of inspectors Gojon had brought with him broke into it through a back door. They took the proprietor of Saint Elvis & Co. down into its cellar.

Fritz had gone to his apartment by then to get some badly needed sleep. Gojon sent me away before going down into that cellar to join Renzo and his inspectors. This was one of those interrogations where he didn't want any outside witness. He intended to get answers to his questions the swiftest way possible. It was at that point three-thirty Thursday morning, and the deadline for Sylvia Vouret was the following day.

I told Gojon I would wait for him at an all-night pub on Saint Médard square, a few blocks north at the end of avenue Gobelins. He gave me a preoccupied nod and descended into the abandoned cellar. I headed up the avenue to the pub.

At that hour people who go to an all-night bar tend to be serious drinkers. The French generally get drunk quietly. But there were some British and German tourists in the place who were being noisy about it. It was a warm night. I took my glass and carafe of Beaujolais outside the pub and settled at a sidewalk table.

For a time I just sat and sipped my wine and gazed across the square at the dark bulk of the church of Saint Médard.

A couple of centuries ago a deacon named François Pâris was buried in its churchyard after dying of overindulgence in torturing his sinful mortal flesh in order to persuade God to bestow His mercy on this erring world. People began coming around to pray for his help: cripples, women unable to conceive children, those with ailing loved ones. Word spread that the dead deacon was performing miraculous cures. Before long there were thousands packed in and around the church, going into screaming convulsions day and night while they prayed for more of his miracles.

The government finally removed his remains to a secret

burial place and put a sign up outside the church: "By order of the King, it is forbidden for God to do miracles in this place."

In spite of these measures, it was quite some time before the *convulsionnaires* stopped having their fits in the square between the church and the pub.

Two centuries, and nothing had changed much. Fanatics continued to commit insane acts to cure a corrupt world. Governments still issued ineffective proclamations in an effort to stop them. I took out my pictures of some of the fanatics who had kidnapped Sylvia Vouret, spread them on the table, and looked at them in the yellowish light coming from the pub window.

Angelina Doniol. Henri Lemaire. Benito Santato. Fernand Claudel. Kurt Seidel.

And a new one. On our way to Avenue Gobelins, Gojon had stopped off at Criminal Records to get pictures of Louis Roy, the ex-con who had introduced Angelina Doniol to the manager of the canal warehouse. I studied the copy Gojon had given me. Roy's face had as much deliberate cruelty as Seidel's and his record of violent acts was worse.

Kurt Seidel and Louis Roy. The charisma of Angelina Doniol must have been powerful for two hard cases like those to devote their brutal skills to her cause.

Her group probably had more members that I didn't have pictures of, but it was dwindling on her. Fernand Claudel was dead, Benito Santato under arrest. She *had* to get Santato free or else carry out her threat to Sylvia Vouret in order to keep those she had and pull in others. You need to build a reputation to become successful in the terrorism business, as in any other.

I put the photos away and drank my wine and pondered

the big question. Where were they holding their hostage? If Jean-Luc Renzo didn't supply the answer to that one . . .

I looked at my watch. It was four A.M. About the same time that they had removed their hostage from the box inside Saint Elvis & Co.

Where had they taken her *from there*?

If the place where they were now keeping Sylvia Vouret was somewhere in Paris, they would have taken her there directly from the barge. At that time of the morning, still dark, there was little chance of anyone seeing them.

Why had they taken her to the shop first?

Because the place where they finally took their hostage wasn't in Paris. It had to be out of the city—far enough away so they wouldn't get there until well after dawn. They wouldn't like the risk of transporting her any distance in daylight.

Sylvia Vouret had been kept inside that closed shop through the following day. It was a weekday, when all the shops in the market were expected to remain locked up tight. They had waited until night—*last* night. And then taken her to where they held her now. Not in the van—not into an area where its Paris plates and odd name would be noticed and remembered. In a less conspicuous vehicle; perhaps one with plates that belonged to the region where they were now.

In a safe hiding place that at least one of the kidnappers knew very well . . .

I was still considering it when Commissaire Gojon drove up and parked at the curb in front of me. He was alone in the car. He climbed out and went in to buy a beer at the bar, then he brought it out and sat down beside me. His knuckles didn't look bruised or swollen. But then I remembered: Gojon preferred to use a telephone book rather than his hands. He kept one in his car trunk for emergencies like this.

You get a heavy Paris phone book landing on top of your head often enough and it scrambles your stubbornness. It doesn't leave visible bruises and, done with control, it doesn't render the victim unable to answer the questions.

"My boys will put Renzo where he'll stay just ours," Gojon said, "until tomorrow. I don't want Emeric or anybody else learning we have him for a while."

"What did you get out of him?"

Gojon took a swallow of beer and used the tip of his little finger to delicately remove moisture from his lips. "Everything he knows."

He said it without any special inflection. But it was one of those occasions when, for just a beat, something peeped out of Gojon's eyes that scared me in ways that the most dangerous criminals I'd met as a public and private cop hadn't.

I reminded myself that I had wanted Renzo opened up as much as he did. Probably more. Sylvia Vouret meant more to me. So did what had happened to Sarah Byrne. Nevertheless, I found myself avoiding Gojon's eyes. And when I looked again, the thing that had peeped out was gone.

He said, "Renzo met Henri Lemaire about a year ago. When Henri dropped into his shop looking for a poster of that old Hitler propaganda film *Triumph of the Will*. Renzo didn't have it, but that started them getting friendly, discovering they had common interests. I told you what we found in Renzo's apartment when we picked him up."

I nodded. Renzo had souvenirs of Hitler and the SS in his private quarters.

"Also, Renzo had a yen for Henri. It didn't come to carnal knowledge, but Renzo was fond of the kid. They kept seeing each other from time to time. A few weeks ago Henri invited Renzo to his apartment to meet Angelina. The idea was to get him to join her group."

"He knew the group was into terrorism?"

"She told him enough to let him get that idea. He said no. The idea scared him. And he didn't like Angelina. Found her too aggressive. Scary. And he didn't care for the way she had Henri wrapped around her finger."

"Did he meet any of the others in her group?"

"No." Gojon looked at me. "Except Sarah Byrne. Renzo's feeling is that she wasn't all the way *in* the group. Like she wasn't sure about it yet. She was acting sulky—jealous of the way Henri acted around Angelina. Henri had to keep kidding her out of it."

"Does he have any idea how many are in the gang?"

"From what Henri told him before the meeting with Angelina, she's got perhaps six people left—without Santato and Claudel and Sarah Byrne. Four men and two women."

Gojon took another swig of his beer and did the trick with his fingertip again. "So Renzo didn't join them. But when Henri asked him for a favor, he went along with it. Because it was Henri asking."

"He let them use his van and his shop."

"Renzo swears he didn't know what it was really for. He thought it *might* be for transporting some weapons. The van was left by someone at his apartment building sometime early last night. With the keys to it and to the shop under the front seat. The way Henri promised it would be. That's all Renzo says he knows about it. I believe him."

"Does he know anything about their attack in the Rue des Rosiers?"

"Only that Henri *may* have gotten the idea for it in his shop. Henri was there one day and made a remark about the street of that name in the market not being the only one. That the other, in the Marais, was full of dirty Jews that somebody ought to do something about. Renzo admits he remembered that when he heard about the terrorist shooting there."

Gojon paused and then got to the only really important point. "He swears to something else I believe. He doesn't know where Henri or any of the others are now. He doesn't have any idea where they're keeping Sylvia Vouret."

I said, "I think I do."

I told him what I thought and then watched him go into a painful inner struggle between the dedicated cop and the careful careerist.

Like most experienced cops, he ended by compromising.

I FOLLOWED GABRIELLE into a wide, gradually rising ravine thick with trees and a profusion of wild bushes and vines. In most places it was impossible to get through side by side. Her family château couldn't be seen from this end of the Lemaire property. It was a couple miles away, with the forested hills blocking the view.

There was a wide dirt path, long overgrown with weeds and brush, leading into this end of the estate from the road. But cars had used it recently, their wheels crushing the weeds when they went through. That increased the likelihood that my hunch was correct. We'd hidden my car and continued our approach to the fortress ruins she'd told me about the hard way.

Hard it was. In places we had to get down on our hands and knees to crawl under tangles of brush. A couple times it proved impossible to get through even by crawling. We had to change direction and circle around the blocked area. Once Gabrielle lost her bearings, and it took her a while to think out a different route. I let her decide. She knew where we were going, and I didn't.

I had been waiting for her outside Taittinger when she'd arrived for work that morning. It hadn't been difficult to talk her into doing what I wanted. Gabrielle Lemaire was more than eager to help me nail Henri. Her excitement showed. Her usual facade of cool, distancing poise was gone. Maybe the weekend with Joel had done her good.

Commissaire Gojon had followed me in his own car with three of his men as far as Reims, but no further. He and his team were now waiting in a Reims bistro. Gojon hadn't told his men the reason for their trip out there. If my hunch proved wrong they'd drive back to Paris, no harm done to his career.

Applying for a warrant to search the Lemaire property would have taken time and alerted Emeric to our intentions—as well as becoming a black mark on Gojon's record if I was wrong. And Gojon was not prepared to trespass illegally on the land of a family like the Lemaires just on a chancy possibility.

If I found out I was right, *then* he and his team would grab a bunch of local cops and move in.

I figured it was better that way anyhow. If the terrorists were in there, there was too much likelihood they'd be alerted by the approach of that many men. I wanted to be close to Sylvia Vouret by then, in a position to do whatever could be done to protect her when the crunch came.

Gabrielle and I mounted a narrow ridge that topped that end of the overgrown ravine. We crossed the ridge and descended into another, smaller ravine, under low trees whose foliage blocked out the sky. I had binoculars stuffed into one side pocket of my jacket and a flat flashlight in the other. I'd given Gabrielle a similar flashlight. The Mauser was stuck in my belt.

I also had a stubby pump-action shotgun hung from my shoulder by its worn leather sling. It had an abbreviated barrel and a pistol grip instead of the normal longer butt-stock, making it a very compact weapon. The four-shot magazine was fully loaded: 00 buckshot.

Gojon had slipped it to me. It had been one of the weapons seized in the capture of a band of bank robbers a few years before. The taking of such weapons is officially noted before they're locked away in a police storage room. Like many officers, Gojon kept some he'd never gotten around to registering in his own private lockup. For emergency uses—like this one.

If I got in trouble with the shotgun, there was nothing to link it to Gojon or his Brigade.

Gabrielle stopped at a dense patch of thornbrush growing against the base of a rocky slope. "There's a little tunnel in there." I didn't have to tell her to keep her voice down. "It's the safest way to get close enough to see the ruins."

I motioned for her to hold still while I listened and scanned the terrain around us. I took enough time to make sure nothing was moving within hearing distance. The field of vision was limited in every direction by the trees, high undergrowth, and nearby hill slopes. But that meant anybody beyond those couldn't see us, either.

When I nodded, Gabrielle pointed to the spot where we had to get through the thornbrush. I began tramping it down as quietly as possible, being careful about the big thorns. But by the time I had tunnel entrance clear, the legs of my trousers were ripped and I had bleeding scratches on both ankles and calves.

The entrance wasn't more than hip high. I crawled in first, using my flashlight. Unless the tunnel forked, I could lead the way through as easily as she could; if it did, she could point. There was more thornbrush just inside. Breaking it down cost me scratched hands and forearms. I crawled on with Gabrielle close behind me. The tunnel cut straight through the inside of the hill with no separations. After several yards it got higher. I was able to get up off my knees and move ahead on foot, as long as I kept head and torso bent.

I thought I saw a dim glimmer of daylight ahead. Thumbing off my flashlight, I stopped to let my eyes adjust and make sure. Gabrielle came up behind me and touched my back.

"It's the other end," she whispered. "You can see the fortress ruins from there."

"Wait here." I stuck the flashlight in my pocket and went on alone, feeling my way with one hand on the rough wall beside me, the other extended.

The tunnel exit was as low as the entrance had been. Very little light came through. It was curtained by thick vines hanging down the slope outside. I went down on my knees and eased forward. Some of the vines were dead; others were thick with fresh leaves. I parted some of the foliage and looked out.

I was halfway up a steep, forested hillside. Other hills rose around a flat area where the surrounding forest thinned out near the ruins of the fortress.

It was more ruin than fortress. All that was left were a couple of sections of straight wall, almost hidden by over-growth, and the remnants of two towers, about equally distant from my vantage point. The top half of the tower off to my left had collapsed, along with one side of the lower half. The tower off to my right was much larger in circumference. It had probably been the main structure of the fortress. But only the base of its wall remained.

They were there.

The used path that Gabrielle and I had avoided emerged from between two of the hills and ended under the ruins. A Volvo sedan with local plates was parked there.

A green tent shelter had been erected against one inner side of the main tower's base wall. Its nylon sides were rolled up this morning. Two men and two women were sitting in its shade.

Inside the other tower, stone steps climbed the shell that was left up to a wooden platform. A man with a rifle was on the platform. It was a good position for a lookout. From there he could survey every approach to the ruins.

That made five people. According to Renzo, Angelina Doniol had at least six, not counting herself. Seven, with her.

Where were the other two?

Getting my binoculars, I inched forward enough to scan the surrounding terrain through them. I shaded the lenses with one hand to prevent sunlight from reflecting off them. Nobody else was in sight anywhere.

I focused on the lookout tower. The man there was Louis Roy. He was taking a turn around the platform, looking at the surrounding hills and the breaks between them. The rifle slung from his shoulder was a long-range Lee Enfield. He sat down on a broken section of wall to light a cigarette. I shifted focus to the low remnants of the main tower and the four there.

A young, stocky woman I didn't know was sitting cross-legged on the ground making sandwiches. The other woman was Angelina Doniol.

She sat with her back against the base wall and her long legs stretched out, talking to Henri Lemaire. The weapon leaning against the wall by her side was a black MP5 sub-machine gun. Maybe the one she'd used at the Rue des Rosiers.

Henri Lemaire was sitting on his heels facing her, an automatic assault rifle across his thighs. It looked like one of the variations of the AK-47.

The other man was Kurt Seidel. He was slumped beside

Angelina Doniol with his head tipped back, apparently taking a short nap. There was a long-barreled revolver in an open holster attached to his wide belt, along with two hand grenades. I could see another grenade on Henri's belt.

Across from them inside the tower's base, near the other side, there was a large round hole in the ground. I couldn't see what was down inside it. The top of an aluminum ladder stuck up out of it, leaning against one side.

I backed up and returned through the low tunnel to Gabrielle Lemaire. I told her everything I'd seen, giving her the positions of the five people within the layout of the ruins. "The hole could be one of the old Roman quarry pits."

She nodded. "The main tower was built over it. I think the fortress used it for food storage. And as a secret way in and out, through the passages connecting to it. When the tower collapsed, much of it fell into the pit and filled the bottom. So it's not as deep as most of them."

"I think that's where they're holding Sylvia Vouret. Are any of the passages to it still usable?"

"One. Come, I'll show you."

We made our way out of the low tunnel. Gabrielle led me through the length of the ravine outside, under the trees. At the far end we climbed a slope and then went down into a deep gully. Near the bottom was the mouth of a cave.

Someone had hacked a path through the bushes that had blocked it. Recently.

The cave mouth was narrow, but high enough for Gabrielle to enter without having to bend her head. I stepped in after her. The interior of the cave spread out a bit but didn't go in very deep. There was enough light from outside to see an opening in the back of it leading deeper inside the hill. It looked like a natural cave passage that had been enlarged into a man-made tunnel.

We started toward it—and then I stopped myself.

There was the sound of someone approaching.

Not through the tunnel. From outside, behind us.

I put a hand against Gabrielle's back and pressed her forward. She looked at my face, and then obeyed immediately, disappearing inside the darkness of the tunnel.

I turned back toward the mouth of the cave, dropping to the ground and snaking forward until I could peer out and see what was coming.

◈ 29 ◈

HE WAS TRAMPLING dry brush under his boots as he advanced toward the cave, a rifle dangling from one hand.

Tall, thin, young. And careless.

I didn't know him, but he had to be one of the other two members of the gang. The one still unaccounted for *could* be nearby.

There was nothing purposeful in the manner of this one's approach. It was just a routine check of the surrounding terrain.

Keeping flat to the ground, I snaked backward and to my left. Then I stood up and braced my back against the wall to one side of the cave's mouth.

He was tall enough to have to duck his head when he came in past me. There was only one way to be sure he couldn't let out a yell. I clamped my right forearm across his throat and swung behind him with my left hand grabbing the back of his head and my right hand locking around my left wrist.

It created a vise he couldn't get a sound through. The rifle fell as his hands shot up to break the stranglehold. By then I had my elbows dug into his shoulder blades so he couldn't. I rammed my right knee up into his lower back, bending him backward and twisting his lower torso to the right while I tightened the vise around his neck and wrenched it sharply to the left.

When I lowered him to the ground his head rolled loosely

on the broken neck. I went flat beside his body and snaked forward again, looked out of the cave. Then I rose and stepped out, listening.

No one else was approaching. I went back into the cave and searched the dead man's pockets. I found spare rifle ammo and stuck it in my own pocket. Lifting his body, I carried it outside and dumped it out of sight under a tangle of bushes between some high rocks. Returning to the cave, I picked up the dropped rifle. It was a Springfield. Good sniper's weapon.

I took it with me into the darkness of the tunnel, snapped on my flashlight, and went through until I reached Gabrielle.

"What was it?" she whispered.

"No problem," I said, and I walked past her. There was no time for discussions of what was already past. I didn't know how long I had before Angelina's gang got edgy about the dead man's failure to return.

This tunnel was higher and wider than the other. It had a steep downward incline. I stopped when I reached a place where a much smaller tunnel forked off to the right.

"We take the little one," Gabrielle whispered. "This main tunnel gets blocked further on."

I had to crouch low going into the side tunnel and stay crouched as I made my way along it. I kept the flashlight pointed down just in front of my feet. Every five or six steps I turned off the flash and stopped to listen and squint ahead into the darkness. Finally I saw a glimmer of light ahead.

I stuck the flashlight in my pocket and reached back to seize Gabrielle's arm, signaling her to stay there. Crouching lower, I felt my way forward until I saw that what was ahead was an opening to dim daylight. Going down on my belly, I inched my way ahead, stopping again when I was a few feet from the opening, able to see through it.

I was looking into the bottom of the pit. Sylvia Vouret sat on the ground beside the bottom of the aluminum ladder, leaning against the curved pit wall with her eyes closed. She didn't seem to have been harmed as yet. She looked the same as when I'd last seen her: a small woman, gone stout with age, her pinned-back hair streaked with gray.

There was a pair of handcuffs chaining her left ankle to the lowest rung of the ladder. That was all, and that was enough. There was no way she could escape through the little tunnel with the ladder attached to her leg. No way I could carry her off through it, either. And no possibility of breaking her free of the ladder—short of shooting open a link of the handcuffs, which would get us both killed by dropped grenades or gunfire from above.

One reason the terrorists had chosen this place to keep her was obvious. It was an excellent setup for them. If they *should* find themselves surrounded by police, all they had to do was disappear into the pit, kill their hostage, and escape via the tunnel, coming out beyond the police cordon and doing a vanishing act.

I was preparing to inch closer to the opening when I heard someone start to climb down the ladder. Freezing in position, pressed flat to the ground, I watched and waited. Sylvia opened her eyes and straightened a bit, looking up.

Angelina Doniol stepped down off the ladder. Her MP5 submachine gun was slung across her back. She carried a bucket in the crook of her left arm and a sandwich in her right hand.

She put the bucket down near Sylvia. "Here you are. Clean toilet."

Sylvia said, "Thank you." Neither cringing nor defiance in her tone. Level, controlled, patient. A veteran of a more savage kind of war than most.

She took the sandwich offered to her and said the same thing in the same way: "Thank you."

"I'll bring you more to eat when Ginette gets back from town with the supplies," Angelina Doniol told her. "And some brandy. You might as well enjoy what you can today. Tomorrow may turn out to be unpleasant for you."

She wasn't taunting Sylvia, just stating the situation in a matter-of-fact voice, and with a firm intention to carry out what she'd threatened when the time came for it. No doubts and no hesitation.

I didn't like something else I'd just heard. The "Ginette" she'd mentioned had to be the other gang member I'd worried about. I hoped she would get back from town well before Gojon and his cops showed up, or well after. A bad situation was going to turn worse if she arrived just in time to spot them and warn the rest of the gang.

Sylvia was looking up at her captor with a polite lack of expression, saying nothing.

"It won't be my fault, what happens to you," Angelina Doniol told her flatly. "Blame it on your government, if they don't free Benito Santato. *They* are responsible for your fate, not me."

Sylvia took a bite of her sandwich and seemed to devote her entire attention to eating it. Angelina Doniol shrugged, turned away, and went up the ladder.

I waited a full minute after she was gone. Then I put down the rifle and unslung the stubby shotgun from my shoulder. Leaving the rifle, I snaked forward with the shotgun until my head was just inside the opening. I pushed myself up on my elbows and watched Sylvia, waiting.

She was about to take another bite from the sandwich when she saw my face there. Her eyes widened. Otherwise she showed no reaction except to look upward quickly. Without ceasing to look up, she nodded.

I held the shotgun with my finger against the trigger when I slid through the opening into the pit. A fast glance up confirmed that none of the terrorists was in sight. It also confirmed what Gabrielle had told me. This pit was no longer as deep as most. The top was less than twenty feet above us.

I knelt beside Sylvia and spoke very low and very fast. "This shotgun is set to fire. If you hear shooting or yelling, get ready to shoot it at anybody who appears up there. Instantly. You work this pump here to get the next shell ready to fire."

Sylvia kept watching the top of the pit as she nodded that she understood. I propped the shotgun behind her. It was short enough to disappear between her and the wall when she leaned back. I scuttled out of the pit and back inside the tunnel.

There was nothing further I could do for her by staying in the pit with her. I could shoot anybody who popped a head over the top, but they didn't have to show themselves to lob grenades in.

My objective now had to be to keep the terrorists away from the pit when the cops arrived.

I picked up the Springfield on my way to Gabrielle. "She's there," I told her, and I didn't say anything else until we were out the other end of the tunnel and into the gully outside. Then I gave her my car keys.

"Tell Commissaire Gojon the layout of the ruins and what I told you about where the terrorists are—especially in relation to that pit. And what arms they've got. Don't forget about the grenades.''

I didn't tell her to remind Gojon to get here as fast as possible. Nor that the cops he brought had to be careful not to alert Angelina Doniol's group before they had the net drawn close enough around it. Gojon had been in these situations before.

Gabrielle disappeared through the woods toward where we'd hidden the car. I figured the time required for her to reach Gojon, and for him to grab some local police and get here, at about forty minutes. Give or take ten. I had to be in position to do my job by then.

Hunkering down, I dug my fingers into the ground. The dirt in that area is like clay. I rubbed enough along the barrel of the rifle to get rid of its reflecting shine. Then I headed for the other tunnel, the one with the opening that looked out on both of the tower ruins.

I sat down on the ground inside the opening, looking first through the hanging vines at the lookout tower off to the left. Louis Roy was still up there on its platform with his Lee Enfield. The best long-distance rifle made. I could only hope he didn't have much practice in using it.

I looked at what remained of the main tower. Angelina Doniol was taking a walk around the outside of its wall base, looking off at the encircling woods and hills. Henri Lemaire was standing and doing stretch exercises, using his automatic assault rifle as a weight. Kurt Seidel was sitting with the young woman I didn't know, eating one of her sandwiches while she leaned close, talking to him.

The Volvo parked near the ruins was still the only car in sight. Ginette wasn't back yet.

I raised my knees to act as a steadying platform when

the time came to do my part of the job. Holding the Spring-field with both hands, I rested my forearms on my knees. But I didn't poke the rifle barrel out through the curtain of vines. No point in taking even a small chance of Louis Roy noticing I was there. Not until I had to start shooting and *make* him notice.

I concentrated on working out the distance and angle of fire between me and the top of the pit that held Sylvia. Gauging how much to allow for both in taking aim. The Springfield might not be as good a distance rifle as Louis Roy's Lee Enfield, but with pinpoint accuracy up to six hundred yards it would do fine for what I had to accomplish. If Louis Roy didn't put me out of action before I could get all of it done.

Angelina Doniol started walking toward the lookout tower, saying something to Henri Lemaire as she passed him. He nodded and picked up a canteen before following her.

When Angelina Doniol called up to Louis Roy, I could just make out the words: "Can you see Raul anywhere from up there?"

"No," he called down, and he laughed. "Maybe he's having his constipation problem again."

Raul had to be the one with the broken neck.

Louis Roy descended the steps to Angelina Doniol. They spoke for a moment, and then he walked off into the woods. Probably to scout around for Raul. Henri was mounting the tower with his AK-47 to take over on the platform. It was their time for changing the lookout.

I'd been handed a piece of luck. An automatic assault rifle is a formidable combat weapon, delivering an enormous amount of firepower in short order. But when it came to distance marksmanship, it wasn't in the same league with a Lee Enfield—or even the Springfield I had.

I waited and hoped for some more luck. I didn't get it.

One of my worst fears came true. An automobile horn started blaring from the woods. It had to be Ginette returning. That kind of noise meant she'd spotted cops while driving back along the forest path.

I tucked the Springfield's stock into my shoulder and poked its barrel through the curtain of vines, aiming toward the pit and remembering my calculations about the distance and angle. The horn kept blaring, getting nearer and louder. Everyone in the ruins was standing and looking toward my end of the path—Henri atop the lookout tower, Kurt Seidel and Angelina Doniol and the other woman in the main tower. Louis Roy was still off somewhere hunting for Raul.

A small Fiat station wagon shot out of the woods and skidded to a halt behind the Volvo. A woman who had to be Ginette leaped out of it, brandishing what looked like a Skorpion machine pistol in one hand. I couldn't hear what she was shouting. At that point I didn't need to.

Kurt Seidel was the first to unfreeze. He jumped toward the pit, yanking the revolver from his holster.

I shot at him and missed. Shot again and got him. He lost the revolver when he fell but he wasn't finished. He did a slow roll near the edge of the pit, a hand reaching for one of the grenades attached to his belt. I cursed and shot him again and he stopped moving, the limp hand falling away from the grenade.

I switched to Angelina Doniol, but she was already at the edge of the pit, starting to point her MP5 down into it, before I could get a bead on her.

A shotgun blast sounded from the depths of the pit. Angelina Doniol went up off her feet and backward as though she'd been yanked by a noose around her neck.

She hit the ground hard, with her body and legs jerking like a beheaded chicken and her fingers clawing toward a face that was no longer a face. Then her arms dropped, and the only part of her that kept moving was the lifeblood pouring from her destroyed face and throat.

A long burst from Henri Lemaire's AK-47 thudded into the slope above my position, bringing a rain of dirt and stones down past the opening. Nobody had told him, or he was too excited to think, but at that range full automatic fire is inaccurate as hell. He should have switched the change lever for single shots to give himself a chance to get me more quickly.

His next long burst lashed the slope just below my opening. If he kept trying, he was bound to hit me sooner or later. But I couldn't even glance in his direction. My job was still to keep the top of the pit clear.

Ginette was sprinting up toward the main tower, getting near to its base wall. The other woman was nearer to the pit, but she hadn't moved from the spot where she'd been when it all started. She was kneeling there now with her head bowed down to her knees, holding it with both hands.

I lined my rifle sights up on the point where Ginette would have to climb over the main tower's wall base to get to the pit. The climb would slow her a bit for me.

Cops emerged from the woods behind and to one side of her, yelling for her to stop, firing warning shots over her head. She should have quit then but she didn't. Instead she spun and fired the machine pistol at them. The next instant Ginette was draped backward across the wall base, her empty hands dangling toward the earth inside it and her feet on the ground outside.

A burst from Henri Lemaire ripped apart the curtain of vines in front of my face. One of the slugs gouged a deep trench along my left forearm. My left hand went dead, losing its grip on the Springfield.

The woman left inside the main tower was still on her knees, bowed to the ground, frozen in terror and shock. I rolled on my right side, awkwardly swinging the Springfield around to bear on Henri's position. Manipulating a rifle one-handed is not working under optimum conditions.

Another hammering burst from him. The slugs buzzed over my head, spanging off the tunnel walls behind me.

Gojon and more of his cops came out of the trees behind the lookout tower. They began firing up at the platform as I finally got a bead on Henri Lemaire.

He went off the platform and somersaulted as he dropped, bouncing when he struck the ground.

A few minutes later Louis Roy strolled out of the woods, handcuffed and escorted by police. He had sensibly thrown down his rifle and surrendered. He'd been inside French prisons before and didn't consider going back into one the worst thing that could happen to him.

Still later, they counted the bullets in Henri Lemaire. There were six.

Only one of them was mine.

⊠ 30 ⊠

SHORTLY AFTER THREE on Friday afternoon I boarded a jet flying south to the Côte d'Azur. There wasn't much about that April in Paris that I would remember with joy. I wanted to put it behind me as quickly as possible, in distance as well as in time.

As we flew over the Alps I remembered the last I'd seen of Jean-Louis Lemaire. Sitting on the ground by his son's bullet-torn body, tears streaming down his face as he sobbed brokenly. Gabrielle Lemaire had stood near, watching him cry, her own face like stone.

I remembered, too, the faces of Maureen and Harry Byrne as I helped them get through the red tape necessary to have their daughter's ashes flown home to California. The fact that they never, by word or glance, indicated that they put any blame on me for what happened didn't make me feel better about it. I was to feel worse, a couple of weeks later, when Paul Rochefort informed me he'd received a check from them for my services and expenses.

But as the snow-topped mountains below the plane gave way to hills running down into the sea, I also remembered something else: the way Sylvia Vouret had clung to me as I led her away from the pit where she'd been held prisoner. And the dazed awe in her voice: "I was so *sure* I was going to die. . . . I was steeling myself to accept the fact that my life was over. I'll never forget what I felt when I saw *you* there—and realized that I might not die after all."

And she hadn't. I had accomplished that much—and *that* was the memory to hold on to.

Late that Friday afternoon I sat once more on my patio with a bottle of *rosé des sables*, surrounded by peaceful palm trees and pines, with the warmth of the Riviera sun soaking into me while I gazed out over the lovely Mediterranean. I wished I could go down into that sea for a long, healing swim, far away from the land. Healing for the soul—but not for the wound in my arm, with its salves and powders, stitches and bandaging. So I had to put off the swim until another day and content myself with just watching the gentle movements of the sea, slowly changing color.

If you do that long enough, you begin to feel part of the rhythm of the sea. You get close to the state that some Indian mystics experience, where eternal, recurring movements of time and the universe become the only reality, with the indecencies and pleasures and tragedies of individuals not really important. The philosophy sometimes tempted me—until I thought about half of India starving because of it.

I thought about phoning Bolivia and trying to get through to Maidi. I resisted the temptation. It would take hours to make a few minutes' contact that would only end up causing us both pain.

I sipped my wine instead and watched the sun go down behind the hills that ran into the sea to the west between Cannes and St. Tropez. Then I watched the moon coming up over the nearer hill to the east between me and Monaco, casting its silvery glow across the darkening waters.

The phone rang in the house. When it rang the third time, I remembered I'd forgotten to turn on the machine. I went inside and picked up on the fifth ring.

It was Nora Darcy.

"Where are you?" I asked her.

"Paris. I seem to have a long weekend ahead and nothing I really care to do with it."

"Get down here, " I told her. "Immediately."

"I'm on my way."

About the Author

Marvin H. Albert was born in Philadelphia and has lived in New York, Los Angeles, London, Rome, and Paris. He currently lives on the Riviera with his wife, the French artist Xenia Klar. He has two children, Jan and David.

He has been a Merchant Marine Officer, actor and theatrical road manager, newspaperman, magazine editor, and Hollywood script writer, in addition to being the author of numerous books of fiction and non-fiction.

Several of his novels have been Literary Guild choices. Nine of his books have been made into motion pictures. He has been honored with a Special Award by the Mystery Writers of America.

STONE ANGEL is the first book of a new detective series.